HAS ANYBODY HERE SEEN WYCKHAM?

The Hollywood Murder Mysteries

PETER S. FISCHER

THE GROVE POINT PRESS
Pacific Grove, California

Also by Peter S. Fischer
THE BLOOD OF TYRANTS
THE TERROR OF TYRANTS
The Hollywood Murder Mysteries
JEZEBEL IN BLUE SATIN
WE DON'T NEED NO STINKING BADGES
LOVE HAS NOTHING TO DO WITH IT
EVERYBODY WANTS AN OSCAR
THE UNKINDNESS OF STRANGERS
NICE GUYS FINISH DEAD
PRAY FOR US SINNERS

Has Anybody Here Seen Wyckham?

Copyright © 2012 by Peter S. Fischer

ISBN 978-0-9846819-7-6

To my lovely wife, Lucille
. . . I love you, I adore you,
I cannot live without you,
you're in my thoughts every moment. . .
and that's just for starters.

CHAPTER ONE

It was twenty-five past one on Monday afternoon, ten minutes after the return of cast and crew to the stage from lunch break, when someone noticed that the passenger in 24A was missing. He sat two rows behind Phil Harris and one row in front of Laraine Day and John Howard. Across the aisle from him in 24D was Jan Sterling. The passenger didn't have much to say for himself. Early 30's sporting curly corn-colored hair, an obviously once-broken nose, not tall and a bit overweight, he was a quiet man who did not draw attention to himself. He was what we movie professionals call "atmosphere". The public calls him an extra. He is actually a bit player with three lines of a dialogue. He sits unobtrusively in his seat, sometimes napping, sometimes reading, sometimes eating but always there. He's been there for the past nine days and now he's not.

William A. Wellman, the director, was the first to notice that 24A was not occupied. He looked around for assistant director Andy McLaglen and screamed, "Where the hell is the guy who's supposed to be in that window seat?" Andy rushed to his side carrying his clipboard and they went over the scene set up.

Andy looked up from his clipboard and called out. "Wyckham! Wylie Wyckham!" No response. He looked around at the others on the sound stage. "Has anybody here seen Wyckham?". Again silence. Andy turned to the second assistant director Phil Puzzo. "Phil, go find the guy!". Phil nodded and grabbed the DGA trainee assigned to the picture, Abe Levitch, and the two of them hurried off in search of the missing Mr. Wyckham.

It is now five minutes to two and Wellman, a man not known for limitless patience, is starting to get very, very testy. I know this is not a good time to get in his line of sight so I shrink back against the wall a few feet from the craft services table and hope to remain invisible as he gimps around the stage, sits, then gets up and gimps some more, checking his watch every thirty seconds. Anyone who dares speak to him at this time does so at his or her own peril. It doesn't help that today is December 7th, the twelfth anniversary of the Pearl Harbor attack and Wellman, a red, white and blue patriot, has been grousing about it since early morning.

The studio is deep into the filming of an ambitious thriller of a movie called "The High and the Mighty". It's actually a co-production between Warners and Wayne-Fellows Productions, an independent producing firm owned by John Wayne and his partner Bob Fellows. The film's plot is pretty simple. Airliner takes off from Hawaii enroute to San Francisco. Halfway there engine problems threaten to down the plane. From that point on it's touch and go whether the plane and all aboard will survive or be lost in a crash in the Pacific. Stealing structure from MGM's hit from the 30's, "Grand Hotel", most of the film deals with the personal stories of the crew and passengers. With the exception of Wayne who plays co-pilot Dan Roman, the cast is comprised of second tier stars and well known supporting actors and actresses. For the most part big Hollywood names weren't interested in appearing in an ensemble cast and that list included such bankable names as Joan Crawford, Ida Lupino, Barbara Stanwyck, Ginger Rogers and Dorothy McGuire. When Spencer Tracy backed out of the part of the co-pilot after initially agreeing to take on the role, Jack Warner threatened to withhold funding unless a suitable A list star name could be signed to the part. That's when Wayne stepped in. He had to.

From the beginning this has been a troubled production. Aside from the difficulties in assembling a suitable cast, Wayne has insisted on filming in the new CinemaScope wide screen format despite objections from Wellman who considers the process cumbersome and unwieldy. For 30% of the film's earnings Wellman changed his mind but my eyes and ears on the set tell me that Wellman remains unhappy. The cast is also unhappy about the cold. December spells winter, even in Southern California, and the heating system on the soundstage is not working properly. Between takes, sweaters and coats are in evidence everywhere. There are whispers of an actor's rebellion if the heating system isn't fixed soon. Claire Trevor, the ring leader of the insurgency, promises she will be heard from.

We all look up as Phil Puzzo and Abe Levitch return from their search. Following them through the door is Harry Davis, the head of studio security. Puzzo whispers into McLaglen's ear and then McLaglen goes to Wellman and whispers in Wellman's ear. Wellman look at him in disbelief.

"This is bullshit!" Wellman explodes. "The son of a bitch isn't Houdini. He's here somewhere!"

At that moment Bob Fellows enters from the far side of the stage followed by his toady-flunky Byron Constable, who reportedly can say, 'Yes, boss, you're absolutely right' in English as well as fourteen other languages, all the while keeping his head in close proximity to his boss's derriere. Fellows, a former director, has been around long enough to know the score and he knows that a company that isn't shooting is costing him money. He strides straight toward Wellman and they start to jaw. I don't hear any of it until Wellman gets to his feet and jabs a finger in Fellows' face.

"And just what in hell do you expect me to shoot? I'm scheduled for a bunch of loose twos and threes, some crossovers and some over the shoulders. I've already established what's-his-name in seat 24A for the past nine days. If I shoot today without him, when we put the angles together, he will be appearing and disappearing in the background like a bunny rabbit on Easter Sunday. Now you see him, now you don't. There he is! Ooops, he's gone. Ooops. He's back! Goddammit, Bob. You know better. Now I'm going to my office and if you find Wyckham, send for me. If not, you had better arrange for a really good photo double or we're going to be throwing away nine days worth of film and paying a helluva lot of overtime!"

And with that he stomps out of the sound stage with that peculiar limp which he has owned since 1917, courtesy of a German fighter pilot who shot him out of the sky over France. More proof that Wild Bill Wellman is a tough old bird who takes crap from nobody. I hope to God Wyckham shows up soon. Otherwise I shudder to think what lies in store.

Now that Wellman has departed I make myself more visible and wander over to center stage where Fellows and Harry Davis are in deep discussion over what to do next. Half the cast members are in their assigned seats either reading or catnapping. The others are wandering about the stage. No one seems perturbed. Like the Army, movie making is a hurry-up-and-wait business. It comes with the paycheck.

"I called his contact number and a woman answered," Harry

says. "She said he wasn't at home and as far as she knew he was at work at the studio. The boys on the main gate says he didn't leave that way and there's construction at the Barham Boulevard gate so same story. Nobody left."

"What do you suggest?" Fellows asks.

Harry shrugs helplessly. "What can I suggest, sir? It'll be a pain in the butt and time consuming but I guess we have to search the premises."

"Oh, Christ," Fellows says. He spots me. "What do you know about this man Wyckham, Mr. Bernardi?" he asks.

I have been trying to get Fellows to call me Joe for a month now to no avail. Maybe it's my new title that has him awestruck. I've noticed that even old pals that go back three or four years show me deference they never did before. It's unnerving and I don't like it much.

I shrug at his question.

"Not a thing, sir,"

"And what do you think about scouring the studio?"

"I don't think there's much choice," I say.

"What about LAPD? Should we notify them?" Harry asks.

Fellows shakes his head.

"Much too early. We may find him accidentally locked in a crapper."

"I agree, R. F. ," the toady Constable says as if someone had actually asked his opinion.

"I'll get right on it," Harry says and strides off.

I can see that I'm about as useful as a blind man at a turkey shoot so I, too, head for the exit. Something tells me that wily Wylie is in one of the unoccupied dressing rooms playing house with one of the secretaries and lost all track of time. Maybe so but in truth I really don't care. I have things to do back at the office. Too many things, actually, but that's the price I must pay for a bigger office and a parking spot right next to the stairway to the second floor of my building.

I've just come down the sound stage steps when the door opens behind me and I hear my name.

"Mr. Bernardi!"

There's no mistaking who it is and I turn to see Robert Newton hurrying to catch up with me. It's Long John Silver himself minus the parrot on the shoulder and the attenuated Aaaaarrr in his speech. In fact Newton, who thrives on playing nasties of every stripe, is a soft spoken cultured man who is a delight to chat with.

"A moment of your time, if you can spare it."

"Always, Mr. Newton."

"Strange business, this disappearance. A first for me and I've been in this business many years."

"A new one on me as well," I say.

"This chap Wyckham. I hadn't realized that was his name. He kept very much to himself. I let him be even though he was a countryman. Perhaps a mistake. I'm not sure."

"A mistake?"

"I had the sense he really didn't feel like chatting, not with anyone and particularly not with me. I think I know why."

"Oh?" I say curiously.

"I tell you this, Mr. Bernardi, because you seem a very genial gentleman with a head in your shoulders and because, aside from taking his direction. the less I have to do with the ill-tempered Mr. Wellman, the happier I'll be. That's between you and me."

"Of course," I say.

"Five years ago I had a major role in the film version of "Oliver

Twist", shot in London."

I smile. "I saw it. You made a dastardly Bill Sykes. Truly loathsome."

"Thank you," he smiles back, "but my point in mentioning the film was not to elicit a compliment. Among the bit players, a patron in one of the tavern scenes, was a young actor named Wylie Wyckham. I remember him quite well because I was fascinated by his name. So Dickensian."

"So then you'd met before," I say.

"Not at all, Mr. Bernardi. The man who has been sitting in seat 24A for the past nine days is not the Wylie Wyckham I remember and I seriously doubt that there are two of them."

"Is it possible you're mistaken?"

"No," Newton says flatly. "The Wylie Wyckham I knew, in addition to being an actor, aspired to being a writer. He was outgoing and quite witty the few times we got a chance to converse. Your Wyckham is as effervescent as flat champagne."

"Strange," I say. "And if true, something that has to be brought out into the open."

"I should think so," Newton says. "And to that end I leave the information in your capable hands. Good day to you."

He smiles and starts back toward the sound stage. I watch him go and then I hurry back to the press and publicity building. I pass by my brand new wine-colored Buick Roadmaster convertible, a present to myself on the occasion of my promotion. And why not? I've worked hard to get here and it's sure far cry from those weeks and months when I was just starting out at Continental Studios with its poverty level paychecks and much deserved inferiority complex. At the top of the stairs I enter through the double doors and instead of turning right as I have been doing for over six years I turn left and head for the large office complex at the other end of the corridor. The name plate by the door reads simply 'Joseph Bernardi'. It should read 'Joseph F. X. Bernardi, Vice President, Press and Publicity', but that's just my ego talking.

I walk in. Ever faithful, always reliable, Glenda Mae is back from lunch and busy typing away at a report I have to give to Jack Warner by the end of the week. Glenda Mae is my indispensable better half without whom I am sure I cannot function. A one time runner-up for the title of Miss Mississippi and homecoming queen at Ole Miss two years running, she has a face like an angel, a figure like Marilyn Monroe and a brain that functions effortlessly at Mensa levels. She knows my job better than I do. Lucky for me she doesn't want it.

She looks up from her typing with a smile.

"Did they find him yet?" she asks.

I'm always astonished at how fast Glenda Mae is able to dial into everything that occurs at the studio, sometimes even before it happens. Or maybe it just seems that way.

"Still looking," I say as I start into my private inner sanctum.

"He called you, you know," Glenda Mae says.

I turn back to her.

"What?"

"Wylie Wyckham. He called you twice. Once on Thursday and once on Friday." She holds up her clipboard."It's right here on my call sheet."

I reach for it and double check. Sure enough, there's his name in two places.

"Why didn't you tell me?" I ask.

"He wasn't asking you to call him back. Twice he said he'd try again. Those messages you don't get."

"I don't suppose he mentioned why he was calling."

She shakes her head.

I'm puzzled but standing there being puzzled isn't going to get things done. I again start for my office. "Get me Cassie Ryan in Casting," I say over my shoulder.

I head for my desk, then pause for just a moment to take in my plush new surroundings. The walls are lined with mahoghany shelves which hold scripts, books, reports, projects finished and unfinished. The leather covered sofa in the middle of the room is both comfortable and expensive as are its companion chairs. In front of it is an antique coffee table. Against a far wall is a television set and two radios, one short wave. My desk is made of teak and was once owned by Huey Long. My chair is on rollers and swivels and was bought new for $1490 at a rip-off joint on Rodeo Drive. The two chairs in front of my desk are padded and comfortable and high enough for my visitors to look me straight in the eye. I am not into power games. I am into doing good work and I will cooperate with anyone who can help me make that happen.

This used to be Charlie Berger's office but my former boss has retired to collect his pension and clip coupons while taking care of his nine year old twin daughters, Daphne and Danielle. I would just as soon wrestle crocodiles than try to raise twin girls alone but Charlie seems to enjoy the angst of fatherhood. Unbelievably he appears to be thriving on a diet of ballet classes, piano lessons, Girl Scouts, and park league field hockey for young girls, aged 9 and 10. He shows no signs of coming back to the studio and that's good because I really like my job. In fact it would be perfect except for one thing and that would be The Man Upstairs. And I'm not talking about God although Jack Warner might dispute that.

My life has changed a lot in the past several weeks. I am

becoming a professional socializer. First Tuesday of the month, it's the Friars Cliub. Second Wednesday, the monthly meeting of the Producer's Guild. I'm Jack's stand-in. The Hollywood Action Committee formed by the six major studios to combat television's inroads on box office receipts? They meet twice a month. I'm the guy from Warners. Charity galas for every disease known to man, I attend them all. Opening night of a new musical or legitimate play headed for Broadway, I'm sitting in Row C, center seats. If I'm lucky I get two nights a week to myself but only if I'm lucky. I tried to fob some of these appearances onto departmental underlings. Warner was displeased. I am the face of Warner Brothers at these events. It comes with the job along with the big title and twice the salary. I used to meet Warner once or twice a week, always in Charlie's company. Now it's two or three times a day on my own and it's starting to grate on me. I'm trapped in a web of cashmere. Disenchantment is creeping into my psyche.

Glenda Mae buzzes me on the intercom. Cassie Ryan is on the line.

"I hear we've got one missing in action," she says as she comes on the line.

"Gone but not forgotten," I say. "Tell me about him."

"I've been going over his resume. Not much here, Joe. Wylie Wyckham, age 33. Born in Manchester March 2, 1920. Trained with Northumberland Theater Group for a year before the war. Unfit for military service due to a heart condition. Performed on BBC radio, had minor roles in West End productions and after the war, appeared in several motion pictures for Rank and Ealing up until 1950 when he formed a repertory company in Manchester. In late 1951 or early 1952 he came to the States where he's been doing mostly stage work in San Jose and San

Francisco. His British credits are decent but he never made much of a living. This picture is his first American credit."

"How'd you find him?" I ask.

"Cattle call. His agent sent him over."

"Who's the agent?"

"Prunella Haworth. She's legit. Worked in the Morris office in London until 1949 when she came here. Went out on her own last year. She's got a couple of dozen clients. No stars but they work steady. I know most of them." There's a pause. "Oh, wait a minute, Joe. There's a little note here. Mr. Fellows office called over and suggested we look at him. I guess that's why I had him come in."

"Was his passport in order?"

"As far as I know."

"No problem with his work visa?"

"No. Why?"

"And studio security took his fingerprints?"

"Yes, it's policy. Joe, what's going on?"

"I have it on reliable authority that your Wylie Wyckham may not actually be Wylie Wyckham."

"Ridiculous," she says.

"Says who?"

"I've got his picture, his resume, photostats of his passport and his work visa. I'm sure his agent will vouch for him."

"And who's going to vouch for the agent?" I ask.

"Now wait a minute, Joe——"

"No, you wait, Cassie. Postwar London was Godawful as the city started to rebuild. There were shortages of everything— fuel, food, housing— conditions were lousy and a lot of people were scrambling to get out. Strange things happened during that time."

"Yeah, but what you're suggesting—"

"I'm suggesting you check his overseas film credits, see if we have any prints here at the studio of any of those pictures and if we do we check out Wylie Wyckham in a projection room. Can you do that?"

"I can try," she says.

"Good girl," I say. "'Call me if you get something set up. Meantime, start thinking about a replacement in case he's gone for good. First thing in the morning, Wellman's going to need a convincing photo double to put in the background before he can resume shooting."

I hang up and take a moment, debating what I should do next. Logically I should do nothing. The missing Mr. Wyckham is none of my business but Robert Newton's disclosure has drawn me in. I'm also troubled by something else. Fellows gave every impression of never having heard of Wyckham and yet Cassie Ryan says that pressure to hire him came from Fellows' office. I think I see the bumbling presence of the egotistical Byron Constable in all this.

I buzz Glenda Mae and ask her to get me Aaron.

Aaron Kleinschmidt is a homicide detective with the Los Angeles Police Department and we go back nearly seven years. These days we're good friends but our first encounter was anything but pleasant as he tried to frame me for a murder I did not commit. Shortly thereafter he mended his ways and transformed himself into an honest hardworking cop. He credits God for showing him the way. I don't agree. I think he was at heart a decent moral man who finally got fed up with being a cog in a corrupt system. Either way he is now one of a handful of people that I trust to watch my back.

"What's going on?" he asks as he comes on the line. "Not

another body, I hope." He laughs when he says it but he's only half-kidding. He knows that I attract corpses the way cow patties attract horse flies.

"Nope," I say. "Missing person."

"Wrong division," he says.

"I need advice."

"In that case, fire away."

I tell him about the disappearance of Wylie Wyckham. I can tell he is only mildly interested. Then I recount my conversation with Robert Newton. His attitude does a one-eighty.

"Newton's sure about this?"

"Positive."

For a moment, there's silence. I know what he's thinking, the same thing I've been thinking. The Red scare is everywhere. Newcomers to our shores are regarded with suspicion and those who aren't who they claim to be are put under a microscope. Joe McCarthy, the Senator from Wisconsin, is waving around lists of people he says are hell bent on turning us into a satellite of the Soviet Union. Meanwhile, otherwise sane people are building bomb shelters in their back yards. No question about it, this is the Year of the Loon.

"You say you have prints?"

"We do."

"This is a little out of my league, Joe, but I know the guy who needs to hear this. Ed Lowery is the FBI's special agent in charge for Southern California. I'm going to call him and tell him what you've told me. He'll probably be in touch with you by the end of the day."

"Thanks, Aaron. I knew I had to tell somebody, I just wasn't sure who."

As soon as I hang up, I have Glenda Mae get back to Cassie

Ryan and ask her to send copies of everything in Wyckham's file over to my office. While I have her on the phone I ask Glenda Mae if there is any news regarding the studio-wide search. Nothing about Wyckham, she says, but security did manage to break up a crap game in the men's room on the sound stage where 'A Star is Born' is being filmed. Also, one of the extras (male) was found in Judy Garland's dressing room trying on one of Judy's evening gowns. . Judy is in New York for a television appearance with Bob Hope on the Colgate Comedy Hour. I have to laugh. I tell her if anything really interesting happens to let me know.

At twenty past three I get a phone call from Ed Lowery, the FBI guy. His voice is crisp and clipped and self-assured, the better to instill confidence that the security of America is in good hands and to scare the crap out of bad guys who might mistakenly think they are dealing with a bunch of Yale educated wimps. He instructs me to messenger my copy of the file to his attention at FBI headquarters in downtown L. A. He will look it over and then forward it by fax to MI6 in London who will run the fingerprints through their files to determine if the missing Wylie Wyckham is who he says he is or, more likely, an imposter.

By four-thirty, turmoil reigns. There is still no sign of Wylie Wyckham anywhere on the studio grounds. Wellman has given up for the day and sent everyone home. He has a casting session scheduled for six o'clock to meet and greet possible replacements for Wyckham. I'll be there but Bob Fellows won't. He and John Wayne are meeting with Mickey Spillane about their next movie, so he's sending his flunky, Byron Constable, in his place. Cassie and her cohorts in casting are going crazy trying to find suitable doubles whose job it will be to sit still and do nothing. Wellman has made it clear that Wyckham's replacement will be not much more than a piece of furniture and will always be photographed out of focus. He has also vowed, should Wyckham turn up, to have the offending s. o. b. tarred and feathered and sent back to the British Isles by rowboat.

I lean back in my chair and take a deep breath. It's times like these that I could really use a nice cold beer but I have an unwritten rule about drinking while I'm working. With the casting session looming in an hour and a half I may not get home until nine or ten o'clock. It may be time to revise my work ethic.

Glenda Mae buzzes me.

"Yo," says I.

"Phineas," says she.

On the phone is Phineas Ogilvy, the entertainment editor for the Los Angeles Times, a bright man whom I count among my friends, even as I regard the rest of the press corps with mixed feelings ranging from tolerance to ill-disguised contempt. .

"What now, my rotund friend," I say as I pick up.

"What, indeed?" Phineas growls. "What's this I hear about Bob Stack being kidnapped off the set of the airplane picture?"

CHAPTER TWO

"You, my friend, have been grossly misinformed," I say to the inquisitive Phineas Ogilvy.

"I am never misinformed, old top," he says. "My sources are impeccable."

"In this case, your sources are full of hooey," I say. I tell him, off the record, about the disappearance of Wylie Wyckham. I don't mention the added complication of probable impersonation.

"An extra?" he moans in disbelief.

"Bit player," I say.

"Same thing," he says. "No wonder that I, who knows everyone, has never heard of him. And you still haven't found him?"

"Not yet."

"Sounds to me as if he's fled the premises," Phineas says.

"You might be right but if so, how he did it is a real mystery."

"And the why. Don't forget the why, old top," Phineas says.

"No chance of that."

"Well, this is very disappointing. I was going to lead with the Bob Stack abduction in tomorrow's column. Now HE would have made an interesting item."

"Sorry to disappoint you, Phineas. Next time we have a disappearance I'll make sure it's at least a featured player with first card billing."

"Gracious of you," he says ignoring my sarcasm. "Meanwhile, let me know if this minor inconvenience turns into something newsworthy."

I promise I will and hang up. A big juicy column about the filming of the picture would be nice but not this column. Warner Brothers is the best of the best when it comes to filmmaking, quick and efficient and always on top of things. That's our message and it's my job to get it out there and keep it out there. Wylie Wyckham, real or otherwise, is making us look foolish and inept. When that happens Jack Warner is quick to call and demand answers. Luckily he is in New York today and tomorrow conferring with his brother Harry. I can only hope he has more important things on his mind.

As six thirty approaches, I trot over to the casting department. Waiting outside Cassie's office are six men with little in common except that they seem to be short and on the pudgy side. They look at me with curiosity as I blow by them and enter Cassie's office. I've already been told that Wellman won't be joining us. The selection of the new warm body in seat 24A will be ours alone to make.

Byron Constable is already there as is a hatchet faced woman of indeterminate age who reminds me a lot of Margaret Hamilton. When she opens her mouth to speak I think maybe she IS Margaret Hamilton but without the charm.

"I believe this meeting as called for six-thirty, Mr. Bernardi," she says, glancing at her watch after we are introduced.

I glance at my own watch. It reads six-thirty-two.

"My apologies, Mrs. Haworth. Next time I am going to be

so thoughtlessly late, I'll call ahead." I throw my most charming smile at her. She hasn't a clue as to how to handle it. If there is one thing I cannot stand it's a smug Brit who thinks she is better than me just because she happens to talk like Wendy Hiller.

"Can we just get on with this?" Constable says irritably. "This fellow Wyckham has cost my company thousands in down time and I don't intend to see it happen again." I am almost amused by Constable's description of "my" company. Bob Fellows would not be amused. Neither would the Duke.

Prunella Haworth draws herself up stiffly.

"I can assure you, young man, that Mr. Wyckham's disappearance was totally involuntary. He is the most conscientious of men."

"And how do you know that, Mrs. Haworth?" I ask. "Are you and he close personal friends?"

"We are amicable," she says.

"And how long have you been amicable?" I ask.

"For quite some time," she says.

"Then you knew him back in England?" I suggest.

She glares at me. "I did not, young man, and I fail to see the purpose of all these questions."

"You will, madame," I say. "You will."

Now it's Constable's turn to look at his watch.

"This is getting us nowhere," he says. "I'd like to select Wyckham's replacement immediately. I have dinner plans with Harry Cohn's secretary for this evening."

"Yes," I say, "we should get this out of the way right away." I emphasize the word "we" and glare darts in Constable's direction. I really don't like this guy. Maybe it's his Nordic good looks, blonde hair, blue eyes, that make him look smug all the time. Or that little red crescent shaped birthmark on his cheek that, so I hear, lots of the ladies find too, too cute. And more likely, it's because he's French-Canadian. As the old joke goes I spent a year one month in Quebec. It wasn't that the people were outright nasty, it's that so many of them were insular, that they believed French Canada was the only place in the world worth living in and the rest of us could go to hell. Sure, I've heard that Constable served with the Canadian Air Force at the outbreak of the war and helped fight the Battle of Britain. I've even heard that he was something of a hero if you can call spending a year in a German prison camp heroic. I guess maybe it is. I sure wouldn't want any part of it. But still, he came out of the war with (or maybe was born with) an arrogance that I can't abide. He's a mass of pretensions, a walking talking cliche with his three piece suits, his antique silver pocket watch on a chain across his belly, his longish sideburns and carefully maintained mustache and wavy hair which he has trimmed each and every morning. One word comes to mind. Poppinjay. However whether I like him is not the issue. I have to work with him and so I will, trying mightily to keep my mouth shut.

"Frankly, I think this whole thing is far too premature," Prunella says.

"I don't," I say. "We need a warm body on the set tomorrow morning at seven a. m. in suitable makeup and wardrobe."

"And if Mr. Wyckham should reappear between now and then?" Prunella asks.

"We will fire him," I say.

"Excuse me," Constable interrupts, "but I don't think that's your decision to make."

"Well, it certainly isn't yours," I say sharply.

Constable glares at me.

"Mr. Bernardi, may I remind you that this film is a Wayne-Fellows production and is not being produced by Warner Brothers."

"And my I remind you, sir, that, according to our distribution deal, every dime you spend is a Warner Brothers dime and we have a helluva a lot to say about where it goes. If you disagree take it up with Mr. Warner and I'll take it up with Mr. Fellows."

That shuts him up and just in time, too, because at that moment Cassie's secretary comes in and whispers something into her ear. Cassie nods and whispers back. The secretary nods and hotfoots it out of there.

Cassie turns to the rest of his with a pleased smile.

"Good news. We've found a print of "Passport to Pimlico" in the film library. We've booked Projection Room Three for seven-thirty."

"We need to contact Mr. Newton," I tell her.

"He's being notified as we speak, Joe," Cassie says.

"Excuse me, but what is this all about?" Constable asks irritably.

"Show time, Mr. Constable," I say "Popcorn available in the lobby. Sorry you can't join us but you mustn't disappoint Mr. Cohn's secretary. Now can we get on with this casting?"

Constable, not one to be left out of any decision making process, calls Columbia Studios and pushes up his date another hour.

Choosing the new occupant of seat 24A doesn't take long. We select a pleasant young man named Sven Lindstrom who's been working extra for several years. With the right hairpiece, the right make up, the identical wardrobe and a camera that keeps his face out of focus, his own mother wouldn't know him. He is delighted to be chosen. He says he hasn't had this good a job since he was macheted to death by Marlon Brando in 'Viva Zapata'. The glamour of the movie business has its grip on all of us.

We reassemble at seven thirty in Projection Room Three. I have grabbed an egg salad sandwich, a bag of chips and a container of coffee from the commissary and am indulging myself in the back row. Supper to me is not a luxury, it's a necessity and I get irritated when I miss it. Neither Cassie nor Prunella nor Byron Constable has brought in food. Their problem, not mine.

Prunella Haworth became properly miffed when she was told the purpose of viewing this 1948 film from Ealing Studios. Unsaid is the implication that she has been duped into representing an imposter and the thought is not sitting well with her. Our projectionist says Wylie Wyckham is the final name to get billing but his character is not identified so we will have to keep a sharp eye out. Robert Newton is the last to arrive and I am delighted to see he is carrying a brown paper bag and a bottle of Guiness. He sees me and heads over, smiling, and takes the seat next to mine. From the bag comes the delightful aroma of English bangers. I nod approvingly as the lights dim and the picture begins.

"Passport to Pimlico" is a silly black-and-white comedy starring Stanley Holloway and Margaret Rutherford. London's Pimlico District, for reasons unclear, has decided to secede from the British Empire and establish its own country. Roads in and out are sealed off. The underground is halted below ground. Passports are required for entry. Exit visas are de riguere for those wishing to leave. Complications pile up on one another every five minutes. For all its stupidity there are times I catch myself smiling and even stifling a laugh. Newton seems to be enjoying it immensely. Maybe you have to be British.

I'm done with my sandwich and start on my chips. The bag crinkles and crackles and Prunella turns and gives me a dirty look. I try to daintily extract one chip at a time from the bag. It's a laborious process. Then I work on chewing noiselessly. Even more laborious.

"That's him! That's Wylie!" Newton says, suddenly pointing up toward the screen. I look. Outsiders are tossing foodstuffs over the wall into Pimlico to relieve the population's hunger after the London bobbies have blockaded the place. A sack of flour has fallen on a young man in a dark colored derby hat and laid him low, covering him with flour. He gets up sputtering.

"Are you sure?" Cassie asks. "How can you tell?"

"Just wait," Newton says.

Sure enough the young man is alive and well in the next sequence with all traces of flour removed.

"That's the chap," Newton says. "Wylie Wyckham. Not a doubt."

"Nonsense," Prunella says. "He doesn't look like Wylie at all, not really."

"Actually, he does. A little bit," Cassie says. "The blonde hair, all those curls done up in a permanent, that's pretty distinctive."

"True, Miss Ryan," Newton says, "but up close the difference in the two men is unmistakeable. And look at the eyes. They're pale, probably blue. The phony Mr. Wyckham had brown eyes, no question."

Constable pipes up.

"We have been duped, Miss Haworth, and Wayne-Fellows is going to find you personally liable for any losses incurred by this situation."

I tell Constable that his pronouncements are not helping matters and to keep his ill-formed thoughts to himself. The picture has been stopped and I point out the character to the projectionist and ask him to splice out a frame featuring a close-up of the actor and then to send it over to the studio photo lab for a dozen 8x10 prints. He promises to hop right on it and the five of of us exit the projection room.

I feel almost sorry for Prunella Haworth who, in the face of reality, has lost her belligerence. She is visibly shaken at having been so easily taken in and I find myself trying to comfort her.

"It's not your fault, Miss Haworth. These are strange times. We were all fooled."

"That's kind of you, Mr. Bernardi, but it was my responsibility."

"I wonder, ma'am," I say, "if you would be willing to show me the file on your Mr. Wyckham."

"Of course," she says.

"Don't you think that's a matter for the police, Bernardi?" Constable says with a hint of a sneer.

"The F. B. I. , actually, Mr. Constable, and I've already been in touch with them and they in turn are communicating with MI6 in London."

This stops him dead.

"You've been busy," he says coldly.

"It's my job, Mr. Constable. Good news or bad I'm going to have to deal with this publicly. Trying to pretend it's none of my business is not helpful. And speaking of not being helpful, don't you have a dinner date with Lizzie Camacho?"

"Who?'

"Lizzie Camacho. Harry Cohn's secretary."

He peers at me down his nose.

"Her name is Beth Littleford," he says.

"That's her maiden name," I say, "the one she uses when she thinks she can get a nice meal out at the Coconut Grove out of some ambitious sucker trying to get in to see Harry Cohn." I look at my watch. "Five after eight, Mr, . Constable. Time flies."

He takes a glance at his watch, throws me one last dirty look and then hurries away. Prunella watches him go and shakes her head.

"I always thought Bob Fellows had better taste than that," she says.

"He does," I say, "but Fellows gets Dr. Jekyll and we get Mr. Hyde. One day Mr. Constable will forget which one he's supposed to be and he'll find himself cleaning out stalls at the Griffith Park stables."

I make a date with Prunella to meet at her office the next morning at ten to look at her files. Properly chastened she has become infinitely more pleasant and I wish her a sincere good evening before I head for home. I remember there's a cold piece of leftover steak in the refrigerator, just enough for a good sized sandwich. Egg salad, tasty though it may have been, is really a dish for little girls and old ladies. My stomach is growling already.

Twenty minutes later I pull into the driveway of my little ranch house in Van Nuys. I have been living here for the past six and a half years and for a host of reasons it's a silly way to live. I am unattached and have no need for three bedrooms. I have no housekeeper so all the cleaning is my responsibility. When a minor catastrophe hits like a broken water line or a furnace malfunction, I have to take off from work and pay exorbitant repair bills to home specialists who charge a day's pay just to take my phone call. I have a yard covered with grass that stubbornly refuses to turn a healthy green and demands water the way a two day old baby demands mama's milk. My so-called garden is a disgrace. The weeds are more colorful than my barren rose bushes. And yet, I don't move. I think it has a lot to do with my childhood which was spent like a vagabond moving from one foster home to another, never being able to put down roots, never being able to say, this is where I belong. And that is why, I am pretty sure, I do not move to something far more convenient.

I pull ahead and park in the detached garage behind my house. Until three months ago there was another car parked there, a 1938 Plymouth owned by my one-time live-in love interest, Bunny Lesher. She's been gone for over two years now. I'm no longer certain why she left me. At first I thought it was to pursue a career. Now I'm not so sure. I think I may have done or said something to frighten her away but if so I have no idea what it was. I have spent tens of thousands of dollars trying to find her because my love for her has never wavered. It still hasn't but there comes a point where common sense has to override blind optimism. I have called off the private detectives. Wherever she is I hope and pray that she is happy and healthy. I fear she isn't but I can no longer afford to pursue this futile quest. What is, is. What will be, will be. Meanwhile her dilapidated car is now in the hands of St. Vincent de Paul.

I walk through the side door into kitchen and flip on the lights. The house is quiet. Everything is neat. No dishes in the sink. No half filled glasses of juice or mugs of coffee on the sideboard. The morning paper has been relegated to the waste basket. I slip out of my jacket and hang it in the back of one of the kitchen chairs. I rummage around in the refrigerator and find my leftover steak. I put it on the counter along with the mayonnaise, a head of lettuce, and a cold can of Coors. I pop two pieces of bread into the toaster and while they are browning I put a placemat on the kitchen table and open the beer. Dinner for one coming up.

Am I depressed? Not really. For the time being I have chosen this quiet, almost monastic, life style. Nightclubbing and bar-hopping were never a part of my social life and I doubt they ever will be. My job allows me to meet attractive and intelligent women and to pursue a relationship if I so choose. I seem to be choosing less and less as the weeks and months drift by but I am by no means becoming a hermit. Tonight I dine alone but tomorrow is Tuesday. Date night. My once a week with the beautiful Yvette and I let nothing stand in my way. So no, I am not depressed.

I sit down at the kitchen table, down some beer, take a healthy bite of my sandwich, and think about tomorrow.

CHAPTER THREE

Bill Wellman is not really happy but he's less unhappy than he was the day before. He has thoroughly inspected Sven Lindstrom and after careful consideration, pronounces him acceptable. He escorts Sven to seat 24A of the airliner mockup and sits him down. I think I heard him say, 'Don't just do something, sit there. '

It's shortly past eight o'clock and they're getting ready for the first shot of the day. The actors and extras are bundled up in coats and sweaters because maintenance has yet to repair the broken down heating system. Claire Trevor is off in a corner of the sound stage jawing with her agent who keeps shaking his head 'no'. This causes Claire to speak even more loudly and angrily and I think I hear a couple of well chosen four-letter words. Byron Constable hears them, too. and walks over to join them, probably with the misguided notion that he can deal with the problem. I hope he doesn't try to bullshit Miss Trevor. I have heard she does not suffer fools gladly.

I'm sitting on a camp chair next to Laraine Day who has been making movies for almost twenty years. Once a gorgeous leading lady who appeared with co-stars like Cary Grant and Gary Cooper and Kirk Douglas and even the Duke himself in the '47 film 'Tycoon', she's still extremely attractive, but she's at that age where parts are hard to come by for even the most talented actresses. I'm planning a piece that will recall all those well known leading men and I want to make sure I'm not treading on any painful memories. She assures me that she adored them all for a variety of reasons and has dozens of anecdotes I can use. Once again she proves my favorite adage. The old stars are the best. It's the young ones who give you the boil on your bottom. I take my leave with a quick hug and a peck on the cheek. Wellman is still working with cinematographer Archie Stout on lighting for the first scene and I see no reason to stick around. But just then Bob Fellows appears. Here's a man I want to talk to so I approach him and pull him off to one side.

"What's the matter, Joe? You look worried," he says.

"Not really, Bob. Just confused. I'm planning on a bang up send off for this picture but to do my job I have to know where the lines are drawn."

"Trouble with Byron?" he says, knowing that's what it is.

"And I'm not the only one," I say. "Tell me about him."

"Well, actually I don't know a lot. Nothng really personal. I met him early this year when we were filming 'Island in the Sky". I was on board a Douglas C47 heading up to Truckee, California, where we were shooting a lot of the scenes and we had a half-dozen reporters on board from some of the Southern California papers. About halfway there the pilot suffered a heart attack and the co-pilot who was really just a kid freaked out. Byron jumped in and took control of the plane and got us safely into Truckee with a beautiful three point landing. That's when he told me he'd been flying Wellingtons for the RAF over Germany and France for at least two years when he was shot down over Bremerhaven in November of '44. He chuted to safety and was picked up by the Germans as soon as he hit the ground."

"Lucky you had him on board," I say.

"That's the way I looked at it," Fellows says, "so I offered him a job. Not much, really. Just a well paid gofer but he worked hard and turned it into something and now he's part of the team."

"I see," I say without much enthusiasm.

Fellows puts his hand on my shoulder.

"Look, I know he can be a pompous pain in the ass but he's a good worker. He's just lousy with people. I'll have a talk with him. Okay?"

"I appreciate it, Bob," I say, trying to make it sound sincere. No amount of talking is going to help with this guy.

I shake Fellows' hand and head for the exit. By now it's past nine and I have work to clear up before I get my usual morning summons from Jack Warner. As I near the stage door, it opens and a very tall man enters, ducking his head so he doesn't bump it on the frame. Those who have never met John Wayne in person really have no idea what a big man he really is. It isn't just that he's tall or broad through the chest, there is something about him that exudes a size that is bigger than life.

"Good morning, Duke," I say.

"Hiya, Joe. How's it going this morning?" he grins as he reaches for his ever present pack of Camels and lights up.

"Getting prepped for the first shot."

"Good. That limey cost us a half a day yesterday. Don't suppose you've heard anything?"

"Not yet."

Wayne looks over toward the Trevor group where Constable is getting an earful.

"I heard from Mr. Slick that the limey may have been a ringer,"

Wayne says. It's the first time I've heard him refer to Constable by that name. Good choice. It fits.

"No question about it, Duke. Robert Newton knew the real Wyckham in England. Our Wyckham is an imposter."

Wayne's eyes narrow as he looks past my shoulder.

"Uh, oh," he mutters.

I turn and see Claire Trevor plowing toward us. Her jaw is set and her eyes are spitting flames.

"Duke!" she calls out.

"Good morning, Missy," Wayne says with a big smile.

"Don't you 'missy' me, Duke," she says. "I've been freezing my tuckus off in this place for over a week and I'm getting damned sick of it."

Constable has been tagging after her.

"I told Miss Trevor we were working on the problem, Mr. Wayne." he says.

"And are we?" Wayne asks.

"Are we what, sir?"

"Working on the problem."

"Well, I assume so," Constable says.

"Don't assume, Mr. Constable, and don't say things you know aren't true. Now get your bony butt out of here and find maintenance and ask them what they're doing about the heat in here."

"Yes, sir," Constable says, not moving.

"Now, Mr. Constable!"

"Yes, sir," Constable says as he turns and hurries for the exit.

Wayne smiles down at Trevor who clocks in at about five feet.

"Okay, Dallas?" he asks.

"Okay, Ringo," she replies with a warm smile and suddenly I'm transported back to 'Stagecoach', circa 1939. Over the past couple of weeks I have learned several things about doing a picture with John Wayne. The most important one for me is the loyalty he shows to people with whom he's worked over the past two decades. Not just stars like Claire Trevor but lesser known supporting players like Paul Fix and Regis Toomey and John Qualen. His loyalty even extends to crew. Andrew McLaglen, the assistant director, is the son of Wayne's frequent and much beloved co-star Victor McLaglen.

Wayne slips his arm around Trevor's shoulder and they walk onto the set. In that moment I am forgotten so I head for the door. I step out into the sunlight and go down the steps to street level when I spot Harry Davis and another man approaching on foot. Harry sees me and waves.

"Joe!"

I wave back.

"Any luck, Harry?" I ask.

"Not a sign of him." He nods toward the guy next to him. "Say hello to Detective Rodriguez."

I put out my hand.

"Joe Bernardi."

"Pedro Rodriguez. Call me Pete."

We shake. He has a firm grip and a warm smile.

"Van Nuys Division?" I ask.

"We got the call about two hours ago," he nods.

"Couldn't wait any longer, Joe," Harry says. "My boys spent most of the night taking a second look. He's gone."

"Something of a mystery," I suggest to Rodriguez.

He shrugs.

"Only if you figure he left the lot willingly. If not, then odds are he was taken out in the trunk of a car."

"Abduction?" I say. "That puts a whole new light on things."

He nods.

"We may need to talk to a lot of people before we get finished," Rodriguez says. "I assume that'll raise hell with your shooting schedule but it can't be helped. "

"Somebody'll have to tell Wellman," Harry says, looking at me hopefully.

I smile at him. "You're the one carrying the gun, Harry. Besides I have an appointment off the lot in—" I check my watch. "—thirty one minutes. Over the hill." I put out my hand again to Pete Rodriguez and we shake. "Nice meeting you. It would be helpful if we could keep this hush-hush at least for the moment."

"I can try," he says. "For the moment."

"Thanks. Let me know if there's any way I can help."

"Will do," he says.

I walk off leaving Harry to deal with Bill Wellman while I gird my loins to face down Prunella Haworth in her lair.

When those of us in the San Fernando Valley talk about heading 'over the hill', we mean taking Cahuenga Pass into Hollywood where, oddly enough, there are no movie studios. Today I'm bypassing Hollywood to reach Melrose Boulevard where I will take a right, drive by the Paramount Studios gate by one block and park near a small but respectable office building at the corner of Melrose and El Centro. It is here that Prunella Haworth maintains her office.

Like the building itself, Suite 203 is not fancy but it is clean, neat and utilitarian. The gold lettering on the glass door reads "Prunella Haworth, Artists' Representative". I turn the handle and enter.

To call it a suite requires a bit of imagination. The anteroom is tiny, dominated by a desk directly ahead behind which sits a white-haired lady who actually makes Prunella seem young.

To the left are bookshelves and a small table on which sits a very short green plastic Christmas tree complete with bulbs (12) and one string of twinkling lights. Three small gaily wrapped faux presents sit by the base of the tree. On the right side of the anteroom are a sofa and a couple of straight backed chairs. There are two offices with doors to the left and right behind the reception desk. Both doors are open. The room on the right is airy with all sorts of seating lining the walls. Obviously, here is where auditions take place. The room on the left resembles a traditional office and I spot Prunella working busily behind her traditional desk.

I approach the receptionist.

"Joe Bernardi to see Miss Haworth," I say.

She looks me up and down appraisingly. I clench my fists so she won't notice my fingernails which I have been biting a lot since I took over Charlie Berger's job.

"You be the fella from Warner's?" she asks in kind of an odd British accent.

"That's me." I say.

She nods.

"Prunella!" she shouts. "He's here!"

I hear Prunella from her desk.

"Mother, for God's sake, use the phone!"

"What for?" the old lady shouts back. "Your door's open!" She smiles. "Go on in but watch yourself, she's in a mood."

I thank her and walk into Prunella's office. She doesn't get up but manages a tight smile as she points to the chair across from her desk. Obligingly I sit.

Prunella nods toward the open door.

"My mother."

"So I gathered."

"I brought her over from England six months ago right after my father died."

"Sorry to hear it."

"He was ninety-six with a bad heart."

"My condolences."

"Mother is ninety-one and healthy as a horse," she says with a sigh of disgust.

"Very fortunate."

"The plan was to have her live her final years in peace with me."

"You're a good daughter."

"That meant leaving her home alone when I went to work. She's clogged the toilet six times, nearly burned the house down twice and when a salesman came to the door she bought 24 toothbrushes and a year's supply of Ipana toothpaste."

"A four year old might be easier to deal with," I suggest.

"Precisely," Prunella says. "So I fired my receptionist, brought Mother to the office and spent two days trying to teach her how the phone system works."

"How's that working out?" I ask.

"Very well, about half the time," Prunella says. "May I offer you a cup of coffee? I make it myself."

"Of course you do," I say, "but thanks no. I've had my morning quota."

"Needless to say, Mr. Bernardi, I am shamefaced about this entire incident. I cannot believe how easily I was fooled by that man."

"One of the hazards of our business, Miss Haworth. We seem to attract more than our share of charlatans and swindlers. Don't give it a second thought," I tell her.

"Oh, but I do and I will, Mr. Bernardi. I will get to the bottom of all this, you have my word on it."

She picks up a manila folder and hands it across the desk. "There's not much here. Mainly his applicaton form to the agency listing all his credits and affiliations. Half of them are flat out lies."

"And you know this how, ma'am?" I ask starting to skim the application form.

"I was on the phone last evening with a dear friend from London. Oliver Watts is England's foremost expert on stage and screen. He is a published author, contributes to 'Punch' and writes theater reviews for the Daily Mirror. Fool that I am I should have called him before taking on Mr. Wyckham. I would have saved myself a lot of grief."

"How so, Miss Haworth?"

"Because he would have told me that Wylie Wyckham was dead. Killed in a boating accident in the spring of 1952 on the Firth of Forth while vacationing in Scotland. Or at least that's what the police believe. His body was never found but there were several eyewitnesses who saw him fall into the icy water from his capsized boat."

I nod, still scanning the application. It's slickly done with just enough believable information to give it credibililty.

"Oliver's going to continue digging for additional information and call me if he gets anything. He believes, as do I, Mr. Bernardi, that the man who presented himself to me as Wylie Wyckham was, at one time, a friend of the real Mr. Wyckham."

I hand back the file folder.

"I agree, ma'am," I say. "Our imposter didn't invent this out of thin air. It has the smell of reality to it."

"That is where Oliver intends to concentrate his inquiries. Friends and associates of Mr. Wyckham in the years before his death with special emphasis on fellow thespians."

I nod.

"Who more likely to steal an actor's identity than a fellow actor?" I say. "Tell me about your Wylie Wyckham, Miss Haworth. What was he like?"

She shrugs.

"Quiet. Polite. Knowledgeable. Talented. He did a passage from Lear for me. Not many 30 year olds can pull that off."

"What about friends?"

"He was living with some woman. It's all in there. Male friends? He never mentioned any."

"Did you sense he was in any kind of trouble? Alcohol, weed, gambling debts, money worries, anything like that?"

"No."

I sigh. Wonderful. A perfectly well adjusted man who either runs away or is abducted by person or persons unknown.

"Would it be possible to get a copy of that application?" I ask.

She nods and gets up.

"The stat machine's in the other room. It won't take a minute," she says.

She leaves the office and I get up and stretch my legs. Behind her desk is a vanity wall displaying a dozen or so photographs of Prunella with the stars of days gone by. Leslie Howard. Conrad Veidt, Edna Best, Gielgud, Cedric Hardwick, Chips Rafferty. She is young in these pictures, young and attractive with no sign of the humorless visage that was to come. I wonder why she never married. In those days she must have had her chances. Maybe the career blotted all that out. No time for a husband, No room for love. There are times when I think I'm falling into the same trap.

She returns with my photostat and I thank her. She smiles and I can see traces of the young Prunella in her face. I wonder if she has ever regretted early decisions she might have made in life.

I pass through the anteroom and say goodbye to Prunella's mother who is standing by a table near the door sharpening #2 yellow pencils. So far she seems to have sharpened about three dozen of them. Maybe she's planning to write a book.

I exit the building and head for my car, the folded photostat in my pocket. I suddenly feel edgy. It is one thing for the ersatz Mr. Wyckham to disappear, willingly or otherwise. It is quite another to learn that the original might have died a violent death less than three years ago. I don't like violent deaths. They seem to crop up around me like weeds in a flower garden. I try to convince myself that my imagination is getting the best of me. It isn't working.

When I get back to my office I find a disquieting surprise awaiting me. Jack Warner is back early from his trip to New York and I have been summoned. I don't know how it happened but somehow I have become Warner's stand-in. Never mind that there are those with more grandiose titles than mine and who have been here two and three times as long as I have, Warner has dubbed me the crown prince. I suppose I should be honored, but given a choice I'd just as soon he honor someone else. Three months ago I started on my second novel but with no free time to call my own I am still in the middle of chapter one. I know I should be grateful for the opportunities I've been given and flattered by the confidence he has in me but a piece of me is getting more and more fed up by this indentured servitude. One day soon Jack Warner and I will need to have to have a serious talk and I am not looking forward to it.

"Good morning, J. L. ," I say cheerily as I enter his plush office that takes up the entire west end of the Producers Building.

"Good morning, Joe," Warner smiles. Then the smile fades.

"What the hell is going on with the airplane picture?" he says dourly.

He's been calling it 'the airplane picture' ever since Wayne brought it to his attention months ago. He vociferously disliked the idea from the beginning but he wasn't about to chase away John Wayne from the Warner brand. So he swallowed his reservations and made a distribution deal that will be good for everyone if the movie's a hit. I've also heard, unofficially, that Warner now likes the dailies and, in a total turnaround, thinks the picture could be a blockbuster. He's apparently looking toward early next summer for release, a coveted slot on any studio's schedule.

In answer to Warner's question, I tell him about Wylie Wyckham's disappearing act but assure him that things are well in hand and we expect no further trouble.

"Well, that's good to hear," Warner gripes. "I drive in this morning and there are cop cars all over the place. Shooting's slowed to a crawl while everybody gets questioned for the umpteenth time. My head of maintenance leaves a message that we need eleven thousand bucks for a new heating unit for the sound stage. And to top it off Wayne and Wellman are screaming at each other on the set about who's got the bigger one. But I sure am glad to hear things are well in hand, Joe."

"The situation seems to have deteriorated since earlier this morning," I say.

"Seems so," Warner agrees.

"I'll get right on it," I say turning to leave.

"Forget it, Joe," Warner says. "There's nothing you can do. Besides I want to talk to you about tonight."

"Tonight?" I say.

"Bill Knowland's coming to town to set up some fundraising

dinners. Take him to dinner and see what's on his mind."

Knowland is one of California's two U. S. senators. He was just re-elected to a second term but the price was high. He owes a lot of money and he's looking to the party faithful to take care of it for him.

"I can meet with him for early drinks," I say, "or dinner tomorrow evening, but tonight is out. I have a date."

"Break it," Warner says.

"I can't," I say.

"Of course you can."

"Very well. I won't."

He looks at me sharply, not quite believing what he has just heard.

"Won't?"

"Won't," I say. "It's a long standing date. I won't break it. Any other time is fine."

Warner glares at me.

"Joe, I don't think you understand the situation," he says.

"I understand it perfectly, J. L. Ninety nine percent of the time I am available to you, night or day, and I'm happy to do it. Tonight is part of the one percent."

"I doubt Knowland can change his calendar," Warner says.

"It's not negotiable, J. L.", I say. "If my decision is not acceptable, you can have my resignation here and now."

"You don't mean that," he says.

"I do," I say, meeting his gaze without wavering.

"What's so damned important?" he growls.

"My business, J. L. Not yours."

I continue to stare him down and I can see the wheels turning in Warner's brain as he tries to figure out what I'm up to. It would never occur to him that I am ready to quit as a matter of principle. In his eyes, such a thing would be impossible. One does not defy Jack L. Warner on a matter of principle.

Finally he shakes his head and shrugs helplessly.

"Okay, I'll talk to his people and we'll try for tomorrow night."

"Thanks, J. L. It'll give me more time to work up a list of fat cat Republicans with more money than brains."

Warner smiles.

"Of course," he says. "I knew there was a method to your madness. Now get out of here and find out what's going on with the airplane."

"Right."

I give him a little salute and leave. By the time I get back to my office I've almost stopped sweating. Did I really threaten to quit? Am I out of my mind? I think of Charlie Berger. Is this what Charlie went through for the twenty-two years he headed the department? I'm amazed he didn't leave the studio a babbling idiot. I am starting to feel very depressed.

CHAPTER FOUR

I leave the office early but I don't need to go home to change. Yvette doesn't really care how I'm dressed as long as I show up with a smile and something in my hand. She's a sucker for little gifts and I love buying them for her. Since today is her birthday, I'm determined to buy her something extra special. I get in my car and drive over Cahuenga toward Beverly Hills. My favorite store is located on Rodeo Drive and it is the only store where I allow myself to shop for her.

I get lucky. A Rolls Silver Cloud is just pulling away from the curb as I drive up and I slide easily into the spot. After I feed the parking meter a half dozen quarters, I start down the street, passing by Tiffany's, Dior, and Louis Vuitton and enter the swank entrance of Bibs & Booties. Rachel, my favorite sales clerk, greets me with a smile.

"Ah, Mr. Bernardi, so nice to see you again," she says. "And how is the little one today?"

"Perfect as usual, Rachel. Today is her birthday," I crow.

"Marvelous! How old? One year?"

"Nine months," I say.

"Then we must find something extra special," Rachel says.

"Agreed,"I say, "but don't forget. Thirty dollars tops. Orders from Mama."

Rachel grins.

"I thrive on the challenge your wife has thrown at me," she says as she takes me by the arm and we start to eyeball the floor to ceiling shelves full of high quality merchandise.

I don't tell Rachel that I have no wife and that I am not a husband but I am most assuredly a father. A couple of years ago I found myself in a relationship with a bright and sassy children's author named Jillian Marx. I adored her but I wasn't in love with her because I was somehow still hoping that Bunny Lesher would come back into my life. I mistakenly believed that Jillian was in it for the fun and the laughs but I was mistaken and when she became convinced that I had no intention of marrying her, Jillian arranged to get pregnant with my child. She was 37 at the time and running out of years. Looking back, I really don't blame her. She was desperate for a child of her own and I was handy. She made it clear from the start that she wanted nothing from me and that she was going to raise the child on her own and there was nothing I could do about it. Early on, there were many tense moments between us but we have worked out our differences and while I will never be acknowledged to Yvette as her father, I am permitted the role of avuncular friend of the family. I settle for it. I don't wish to give anyone grief.

"What do you think?" Rachel asks.

"What?" I'm awakened from my thoughts.

"I think it's perfect," she says, holding up the small sterling silver cereal bowl. It is girded with colorful ceramic Pooh characters and comes with a matching spoon featuring Christopher Robin.

"You're right," I say with a smile. "How much?"

She shrugs.

"Forty nine dollars," she says helplessly.

Now we play the game. I give her forty-nine dollars cash leaving no paper trail. She retags it at $29.95 and gives me a receipt for the same amount. She gift wraps it leaving the receipt in the box and the tag on the bowl. Now everybody will be happy.

Jillian still lives in her fashionable old house built into the side of a hill on Franklin Avenue and I pull up to the curb in less than fifteen minutes. I can see a gorgeous Christmas tree framed in the front window and a faux Frosty the Snowman waves at me from the front yard. I wave back. As I jog up the steps, Jillian opens the front door and greets me with a smile. I give her a quick hug and a brotherly peck on the cheek as we go inside. Immediately I smell garlic. Lasagna's on the menu. Excellent. There are half a dozen Italian restaurant chefs in swank Beverly Hills who could use cooking lessons from Jillian.

"How's the new job?" she asks as we head into the living room.

"Great," I say, dripping sarcasm by the cupful. "I've been promoted from a happy-go-lucky productive assistant into a weary, depressed flunky with no life of my own. Galley slaves had it better than me."

"Ah," she says, "at last, a peek at the real Jack Warner."

"More than a peek, my dear," I say.

And then I spot Yvette, sitting in the middle of her playpen, trying to pull the ears off of Bucky Bear, one of Jill's literary creations turned into a stuffed animal for tots. I kneel down by the slats and peer in, waving my fingers at her.

"Happy birthday, Yvette," I say.

She looks up at me, gives me a suspicious once over and returns her attention to the bear. I'm miffed.

"What did I do wrong?" I whine.

"Nothing," Jill says. "Bucky is her new best friend and she won't be satisfied until she tears him apart." She puts out her hand. "Let's have a look."

I hand her the gaily wrapped present and she opens it methodically, determined to save both paper and ribbon. Then she removes the box lid and takes out the bowl, examining it appreciatively.

"Lovely, Joe," she says.

"I'm a good shopper," I say.

Now we start part two of the little charade. She knows I spent more than thirty dollars on the bowl but as usual, she pretends otherwise.

"You have a wonderful eye for a bargain." she says.

"It was a close-out," I say.

"A close-out. Of course. Well done, Joe. Tomorow morning I'll christen it with her pablum."

"I'd love to be there to see that," I suggest by way of a feeler.

"I'm sure you would," she smiles. This is Jillian-code for "Fat chance."

I sigh inwardly. Sex is no longer part of our relationship. She has a couple of casual male friends who pitch in when needed. I have a couple of willing young ladies I can wine and dine and bed when the urge becomes great. I guess she has it right. Bunny is now and always has been a wedge in our relationship so why tempt fate. The last thing either of us wants is a rupture in our loveless but genuine friendship. With my access to Yvette at stake, I play along. Whatever Jill wants, Jill gets.

Dinner is superb. Jill and I chat easily. Yvette sits in her padded high chair, dipping her hand into a bowl of milk-soaked Kix and occasionally managing to get one or two of them into her mouth. I tell Jill about the mysterious Mr. Wyckham. She tells me about feelers her publisher has been getting from George Pal for a full length animated version of her new book about a singing salamander.

I am in the process of scraping my plate clean of the remnants of my lasagna when Jill spoons out a substantial second helping. Between that and the garlic toast and the bleu cheese salad, I am eating like royalty or at the very least, a politician. I know one thing. It beats hell out of a steak sandwich and a bag of chips.

We're in the middle of tiramisu and cappuccino when she comes out with it and I never even saw it coming.

"How's your Saturday?" she asks.

"Don't know. Probably a lot like every other Saturday. Why?"

"I need a favor," she says. Odd. Usually when she's after something from me she circles it for fifteen or twenty minutes before getting to the point.

"Sure," I say.

"You don't even know what it is."

"Don't care."

"Bridget left for Ireland this morning."

Bridget is Jill's ancient but still mobile housekeeper/governess.

"Happy to pitch in," I say, "but I don't do windows."

"Her mother's getting married this weekend. She'll be gone until next Tuesday." I look at her in disbelief. Jill throws up her hands helplessly. "Bridget is 63. Her mother is 87. She's been living with this sheep rancher for six years. The parish priest finally gave up and threatened her with eternal damnation. She didn't care but the sheepman did. The entire village will be there."

"I'm not surprised."

"Saturday I have to be in Sacramento for a book signing. I would like to beg off but Governor Brown's going to be there along with his 8 year old daughter Kathleen who just "adores" Henry Hedgehog and insists on meeting me. With a gun to my head I am going. Afternoon flight there, Sunday morning flight back."

"And naturally, you are not going to take a nine month old child on an airplane any more than you would let her sleep in a rented crib in a hotel room."

"Precisely."

"So you want me to disrupt my well-ordered life and come over here on Saturday where I will have to tend to the child by myself for at least eighteen hours." I screw my face up into a scowl.

She laughs.

"Is that the best you can do?"

"Wait, let me try again," I say. I make another attempt but it's no better. I am fooling no one. She laughs. I laugh. I reach across the table and kiss her on the cheek. I know how hard this must have been for her and I am grateful. It's not the asking that was hard but the idea of, in a very small way, giving me more access to my child.

"Just this one time, Joe," she says.

"Of course, :"

"We can't make a habit of this."

"We won't."

We smile at one another and then look over at the baby. Yvette looks at us and suddenly slams a little baby fist into the bowl of milk turning it upside down and soaking herself in the process. For a moment she is startled and then she starts to giggle joyously. I look at Jill who looks at me and then we start to giggle as well. Ah, parenthood. There's nothing like it.

At 8:15 we put the baby to bed. Jill thanks me for coming by and for my Saturday night commitment but makes it clear this evening is finished as she has work that needs her attention. I tell her I understand, give her a hug and take off.

On the way home I scan the radio for something worth listening to. For a week now I've been avoiding the barrage of Christmas songs that assault me twenty four hours ago because frankly, I haven't felt very Christmasy. Partly because this the time of year I think most about Bunny, partly because Christmas was never much a part of my childhood, and partly because the independence I cherish during the year turns to loneliness when the calendar flips to December.

But thinking about the Saturday to come, everything changes. I find myself smiling and at one point I start to sing along, fumbling with lyrics I haven't really listened to for years. When I finally get home and climb into bed, I forget all about Wylie Wyckham and Prunella Haworth and the C-54 mockup on Stage 12 and yes, I even forget about Jack Warner. Sleep claims me.

CHAPTER FIVE

The following morning it all comes back to me. Wylie Wyckham and Prunella and the C-54 on sound stage 12 that just sits there and goes nowhere. And, oh yes, Jack Warner who had me in his office at 9:15 with a crisis on his hands which he was soon to put in my hands. He has decided to release "The Eddie Cantor Story" on Christmas Day so that it will qualify for the Academy Awards. I am aghast and already feeling little waves of nausea lapping over me like the incoming tide at Malibu Beach.

The movie is an ill-conceived project which in theory will emulate the huge success of Columbia's 'The Jolson Story'. Never mind that the Jolson picture came out six years ago and is already a distant memory. Never mind that the screenplay is pedestrian at best and never mind that a young and relatively unknown actor named Keefe Brasselle gave the Cantor impersonation the old college try but came up very, very short. Warner, on the other hand, thinks he has an Oscar contender on his hands and it will be my job to bang the drum loudly to persuade the press and the public that this pipsqueak of a picture has a fighting chance of beating out this year's presumptive winner for Best Picture, "On The Waterfront". It is times like these that I hate my job.

I glance at my watch. 10:33. I have been sitting here for the past thirty minutes conceiving and then discarding a dozen ways to draw America's attention to this movie. An obvious approach is to book Brasselle on several of the network variety shows but if I do, they'll probably ask him to sing and I'm not at all sure it's Brasselle's voice I heard on the soundtrack. We could stage a series of non-singing press conferences but these are usually lame affairs and not likely to be well attended, especially considering we are in the midst of Christmas season.

I decide to lay the whole thing off on Dexter. When I became Charlie Berger, Dexter became me and took over my office at the other end of the corridor. He is a tireless go-getter who knows how to think and I like him a lot. I'm pretty sure he likes me as well. However I doubt that the feeling will persist after I drop this wagonload of manure in his lap. I buzz Glenda Mae to get him for me. A minute later she buzzes me back and tells me Dexter is out in Palmdale on location with the bug movie. It's actual title is 'Them' and it's about a bunch of ants on steroids going up against the likes of James Whitmore and Jim Arness. For all the kidding we do, though, the dailies have been excellent and for what it is, I think it's going to be a pretty good drive-in programmer. Too bad it can't be ready in time for that Christmas Day release date.

I tell Glenda Mae to leave word with Dexter's secretary that I want to see him as soon as he returns and then I lean back in my chair and at long last begin to contemplate something that has been bothering me ever since I first heard about it. Last Thursday Wylie Wyckham called me here at my office. I was out. He left no message. On Friday he called again and again I was out of the office. And again he left no message. This is a man I did not know and had never met so I have no clue as to why he wanted to talk with me. I do know one thing, however. On Monday he left the set for lunch and never returned and where he is, nobody knows. My curiosity is starting to itch like a bad case of heat rash.

I open the middle drawer of my desk and take out Wyckham's application to the Haworth agency. Under "Emergency Contact" I find the name Phoebe Sweets, same address, same phone number. Most likely a live-in gal pal. I buzz the phone number to Glenda Mae and ask her to get Miss Sweets on the line. A minute later she double buzzes me and I pick up.

"Good morning," I say. "Is this Phoebe?"

"It is," comes this soft lilting almost child-like voice.

"This is Joe Bernardi from Warner Brothers Pictures."

"Oh, my!" she says as if I'd just introduced myself as the Pope.

"I hope I haven't caught you at a bad time."

"Oh, no, sir. Not at all. Have you found Wylie?"

"I don't think so but I'm not part of the search party. I work in publicity."

"Oh, my!" she says again even more impressed.

"I was hoping you might have a few minutes to sit down and chat with me."

"I certainly do," she says. "I'm not due at work until noon. Please come by. I will be so honored to meet you."

Really? I can't think why but I verify her address and tell her I will be there before 11:00.

Phoebe Sweets lives in a seedier section of Venice, a beach community just south of Santa Monica. Seedy is a relative term when it comes to Venice. It used to be a well known tourist attraction with its pier and the rides and the dozens of canals so reminiscent of its namesake in Italy. But time has been unkind to this little enclave with its decaying ocean front walk and its pot-holed streets and alleys. It is home to hundreds of cash poor poets, struggling writers and unemployed actors and directors. They'll tell you they live here for the ambience but it's the rent.

I park directly in front of Phoebe's weather beaten bungalow and lock the car up tight. If there be vandals about I don't see them but I take no chances. I will be sitting by Phoebe's front window with one eye on the street. So far my gorgeous new Buick hasn't a scratch on it. I intend to keep it that way.

I knock on the door and it is immediately opened by a smiling dark haired woman wearing a flowing caftan which I immediately suspect is trying to hide some excess weight.

"Come right in, Mr, Bernardi," Phoebe says. "I am so delighted to meet you."

"And I you," I smile as I enter. The living room is tiny. I can see through to the kitchen. It is tiny. So, I suspect, are the bedrooms and the bathroom. Everything about this place is small except for Phoebe. I notice that there is a tea service on the coffee table along with a small plate of cookies. Phoebe plans to ply me with food and drink.

"Please sit down, Mr. Bernardi. May I offer you tea?"

"Certainly," I say. "Milk, one sugar."

She pours. I study her carefully. She is not unattractive except for the poundage. Her smile is genuine and very pretty blue eyes peer out at me from her roundish face. She hands me my tea and then begins to sing.

"For TV Live, it's Channel Five. A time to work and a time to play. Start your day with KTLA. Doot-doot-dootle-dootle-doo!"

She smiles at me expectantly.

"Well?" she says.

"Well what?"

"The jingle! That's me. Don't you watch Channel Five?"

"Oh, sure," I say. "Very nice. Did you write it, too?"

"No, our Mr. Crabtree wrote it. He's a genius."

I nod appreciatively. Geniuses are hard to find these days/

"So you work for KTLA," I say.

"Over two years now."

"And you sing jingles?"

"Oh, yes. And I dance sometimes. I'm the Old Gold cigarette pack on the Friday 7:30 talent show."

I nod as if I've seen it which I haven't.

"And then, of course, I have to do a lot of other things like typing and filing and answering the phone but I really don't mind because it gives me a chance to pursue my real career."

I smile.

"Good for you," I say. "Now tell me about Wylie."

"Well, let me see," she says, pouring her own tea. "We met a year ago when he came to the studio to read for the part of a mailman on 'Life With Elizabeth'. That's Betty White's show. I know you've seen it."

"Oh, yes," I lie again. Who the hell is Betty White?

"He didn't get the part. Just because he had this slight British accent. I thought he was wonderful. Well, anyway we had gotten to chatting and then he asked me to lunch and I found out he'd been in the city only a short time and really hadn't been working much and he'd just been evicted from his apartment—"

"And one thing led to another and you invited him to stay with you," I suggest.

Her eyes widen, totally surprised.

"How did you know?" she asks.

"Lucky guess."

I pluck a cookie from the plate and glance out the window at my car. Still safe. Phoebe rattles on. At first Wylie occupied the sofa. Then he found his way into her bed. She giggles as she talks about this. His days were spent looking for work mostly without success. Phoebe took care of the grocery shopping and the rent and most importantly, the booze bill. A couple of nights a week he'd be out until late but most evenings they would sit and watch television and toss back a few whiskeys. Invariably he would mock the actors on the dramatic shows. Jealousy, no doubt, she thought.

"And during all this time, did he ever find work?" I ask.

"No, he didn't," she says, " and I can tell you why. The hair and the nose."

I look at her puzzled.

"The hair and the nose, Mr. Bernardi," she says. "When I first met Wylie he was such a handsome man with beautiful thick brown hair. Well, about a week after he moves in, he comes back one evenng with this huge bandage over his nose and his hair, oh, my God, it was just dreadful. All cut kind of shortish and bleached blonde and then curled like he'd gotten a permanent. When I asked him what happened, he said he was changing his look, trying to get character parts. That's why he'd had his nose broken. He had such a beautiful nose, I was just beside myself, but there was nothing I could do about it. And oh, yes, he'd gotten rid of his glasses as well. Got himself those little things you put in your eyes—"

"Contact lenses."

"That's right. Oh, my God, Mr. Bernardi, it was like I was suddenly living with a whole different man."

"And then this whole different man, was he able to find work?"
She shakes her head.

"No. Or at least not until three weeks ago when he got this job at your studio, working on the airplane picture. I remember how proud he was when he walked in. He smiled at me and reached in his pocket and took out this roll of bills and peeled off three hundreds and put them in my hand. For everything I'd done for him. The studio had given him an advance on his paycheck and he wanted to share with me. What a lovely thought, don't you think, Mr. Bernardi?"

I agreed that it was even as I am trying to figure out what nitwit in payroll gave him an advance on his salary, something that is not done. Not ever. Not even for Jack Warner.

"You know, I don't want to alarm you, Miss Sweets—"

"Phoebe," she smiles.

"Phoebe," I correct myself, "but the police are beginning to think that Wylie's disappearance from the set was not voluntary."

"Oh, no," she says. "It was his idea all right."

"What makes you so sure?"

"Because he took everything with him."

"When was this?" I ask, very confused.

"That Sunday night. Maybe Monday morning. We'd really been going at the booze hot and heavy and to tell you the truth, I don't even remember getting into bed, but that's where I woke up around eleven o'clock in the morning with a helluva headache. I mean a killer like I'd never had before. The first thing I noticed was that all his clothes were missing from the closet. So was his suitcase. I looked around for a note but there wasn't any. Of course, I was very upset but I really didn't know what to do so I just waited. That evening when I got home from work one of my neighbors told me the police had been around. I found a business card had been shoved through my mail slot. It was a detective named Rodriguez so I called him and that's when I found out that Wylie was missing."

I drum my fingers nervously on the arm of my chair.

"Did you tell Rodriguez about Wylie's moving out?"

"Yes, I did."

"What did he say?"

"Nothing."

I drum my fingers some more.

"Phoebe, can you think of any reason why Wylie would just suddenly pack up and leave?"

She looks at me sadly.

"None I'd care to dwell on," she says and I know what she's thinking, that Wylie, having come into some money, no longer needed nor wanted her company.

"Tell me about his friends," I say.

"He didn't have any," she says.

"None?" I say incredulously.

"None I knew of," she says. "Like I said, once or twice a week he'd go out and wouldn't come back until late but I have no idea where he went or who he was with." She glances at her watch. "Oops. Time for work."

She gets up. So do I.

"One last question, Phoebe. Twice Wylie called me at my office at the studio but didn't leave a message. Do you have any idea what that was about?"

"Not really. He talked a lot about getting some press notice for his part in the picture even though his part was small. He said he had a lot of funny stories about movie making in England. Maybe that was it."

"Maybe," I say, unconvinced.

I try to shake her hand. She tries to gjve me a hug which is when I realize there's a lot of Phoebe underneath that caftan.

"You're a lovely young lady, Phoebe Sweets, and I don't want to alarm you but on the other hand, I don't want anything to happen to you, either."

"My goodness, Joe, what ARE you talking about?"

"Just that your Wylie is missing under mysterious circumstances and we don't know why. It's possible that those who knew him best might also be in some sort of danger."

"Oh, pooh," she laughs. "You can't be serious."

"But I am. Keep your doors locked, Phoebe, and be careful about who you let in. I'm going to ask Detective Rodriguez to arrange for a little extra surveillance for the next few days just in case."

Again she laughs. She thinks I'm making something out of nothing but when I hand her my business card with my home number scrawled on the back she promises to call me if anything else occurs to her.

On the way back to the studio I give a lot of thought to Wylie's departure from Phoebe's bungalow less than 24 hours before his disappearance from the set. Is there a connection? I'd bet my pension on it which is not as rash as it sounds since I won't be vested for another four years. I think about spending another four years with Warner and my Christmas spirit starts to melt away like the Wicked Witch in 'The Wizard of Oz'.

As I walk into my office, Glenda Mae reminds me that I have a dinner date this evening with Senator Knowland. The Polo Lounge at the Beverly Hills Hotel where Knowland is staying. Eight o'clock sharp. I sigh. Another perfectly good evening shot.

I have Glenda Mae call the commissary and have them send up a club sandwich with chips on the side. Then I dig out my private little phone book and write down three names with their phone numbers. When my sandwich arrives I tell Glenda Mae to take an hour and half for lunch. If that gives her time for a nooner with her husband Beau, so be it, but I don't want her back here until at least two-thirty. Before my sandwich arrives I call the payroll department. They tell me what I already know. No advance salary for Wyckham. Now my curiosity is really aroused.

There's a knock on my door and Rhoda, the cute little brunette from upstate New York enters with my lunch. I flirt with her shamelessly and she gives as good as she gets and I make a mental note that she is someone worth further investigation.

As soon as she leaves I make the first of my three phone calls. By two-twenty I will have finished the third and I am pretty proud of myself. All three are what Vegas calls "whales" Very very rich and easily separated from their money if the reason is right. In this case the reason is unassailable and all three, Republicans to the core, will be on the hook for massive sums to bail Knowland out of debt. I have not made these calls through the company switchboard. There is no record of them in Glenda Mae's logs. The phone I have called on has been contracted for under the name Charles Foster Kane. I pay the bill, sent each month to a post office box, by money order. Since it is highly likely that my whales and the Senator will be soon breaking a half dozen campaign finance laws, I have separated myself the best I can from their chicanery. How did I get so smart and so cautious? Charlie Berger. Twenty two years on the job and not one subpoena. I learn from the best.

At two thirty, Glenda Mae is back. I check her out and see that her dress is not mussed and neither is her makeup which means she used her extended lunch hour to actually have lunch. I head for the door and tell her I'll be on the set if Warner calls. If Rodriguez is there I want to know what he thinks about Wyckham's moving out of Phoebe's bungalow. I think it sounds relevant but I'm not a cop. I could be all wet.

I strut down the staircase and head for the sound stage at a brisk pace. In my world, this constitutes exercise. The fresh air is a bonus. As I turn toward the stage a stout woman in a blue skirt and jacket is striding toward me. She isn't fat so much as solid. I look at her. She looks at me. I look away. She looks away. I pass her by and then I hear my name.

"Bernardi?"

I turn and she's stopped, regarding me quizzically.

"Joe Bernardi?" she says.

"That's me," I say.

She walks up to me, jaw set in concrete.

"My name is Bertha Bowles and I want to know why you're giving my client the shaft."

CHAPTER SIX

Ma'am?"

"Don't you 'ma'am' me, buster," she says. Bertha Bowles isn't tall and she isn't fat. She's substantial and solid and shaped like a rectangle and I'd think twice before getting into an arm wrestling contest with her. Her hair is black with streaks of grey and her makeup is minimal. The shoes on her feet are flat and sensible.

"I really don't know what you're talking about, Miss or I mean, Mrs. —"

"It's Miss Bowles and don't you forget it," she says. "You do a long puff piece for the Times on Claire Trevor, another one on Jan Sterling for the Herald Express, you even write up Julie 'Who the Hell is She?' Bishop for the San Diego Union Tribune.

"Who's your client, Miss Bowles?" I ask.

"I manage Bob Stack."

"Oh."

"What do you mean, oh? What's that supposed to mean?"

"I haven't approached Mr. Stack because I wanted to touch base first with Wellman and Wayne. You know your boy wasn't first choice for this role."

"Yeah, they wanted that pretty boy Cummings. Lucky for

your film the two geniuses changed their minds."

I shake my head and can't surpress a smile.

"You know, Miss Bowles, I've always been taught that agents and managers best serve their clients by being cooperative and circumspect. You seem to have developed a different approach."

"Damned right, Bernardi. Listen, you let people push you around and you won't be in the business long, especially if you're a woman. I may scrape a few egos but nobody ignores me. So what about Stack?"

"Well, for one thing, he's doing a bang up job and if it were totally up to me, I'd be releasing a lengthy Q&A piece complete with photos and then I'd be talking to Photoplay about a cover story. But in the real world I have to run it by the Duke."

She regards me with suspicion.

"You wouldn't jerk around an old lady, would you, Joe?" she asks.

I make a show of looking to my left and right.

"Why? Is there one here?" I ask, pokerfaced.

She smiles and shakes a finger at me.

"Very slick. I heard you were a smooth article."

"Like a baby's butt," I say. "And I heard you were a tough old bird."

She nods.

"Part vulture, part buzzard and one hundred percent mule. Best you take my word for it."

"I'll do that, Bertha," I tell her.

"And Stack?"

"I'll talk to Wayne before they wrap for the day."

"Okay. So how's Charlie doing?" She's talking about my retired boss, Charlie Berger.

"He says good."

"You believe him?"

"Not sure."

Bertha shakes her head.

"Twenty two years of taking crap from that egotistical blow-hard. I can't believe Charlie got out alive. How about you, Joe? You ready for your twenty two years?"

"I'll be okay," I say.

"I hope you're not counting on Jack Warner quitting or dying. Neither one is part of his nature."

"We get along just fine," I say.

"So do we, said the spider with his arm around the fly." She smiles again and jabs her hand in my direction. "Good luck, Joe. Nice chatting with you."

"My pleasure, Bertha," I say.

Her grip is firm and then she turns and heads off toward the visitor's parking lot. I continue on to the sound stage. The warning light over the stage door is unlit so I'm free to enter.

Going from sunlight to the dark of the stage, I'm momentarily blinded and almost stumble over a three foot tall bundle of energy who darts in front of me playing with a toy airplane. Michael Wellman is the director's eight-year-old son and he plays a kid named Toby traveling alone from Honolulu. Put on the plane by his father, he will be met by his mother in San Francisco. He's Wellman's only major deviation from Ernie Gann's book and I think it's a good one. Toby will fall asleep before the crisis erupts and won't wake up until the plane is safely on the tarmac in San Francisco. It's an interesting grace note and will play well against the tension of the rest of the film. Even Gann approves, .

Wayne has changed into his co-pilot's uniform and in the scene they are shooting, he has come back into the cabin area to reassure the passengers. But my attention is focused on the far corner of the sound stage where I see Pete Rodriguez, the detective from the Van Nuys Division, quietly questioning Phil Harris. Harris is a man of many talents, a one time bandleader, second banana on The Jack Benny show for several seasons and now the co-star along with his wife, Alice Faye, on the most popular show on radio. He's juggling this film along with his radio commitment and so far he seems to be getting away with it.

I make a beeline for Wayne and pull him aside. When he hears my problem, he just grins.

"You don't need my permission to do your job, Joe. Stack's terrific. Do what you want. Anything to help Bob as well as the picture."

"That's what I thought you'd say. Just double checking."

Wayne glances over toward Rodriguez and then back to me.

"So what's the latest on Wyckham?" he asks.

"Nothing, as far as I know. It's like he disappeared down a huge gopher hole," I say. "How's Wellman feel? Is he happy?"

"He's never happy, at least not so's you'd notice. But he'll be okay."

We hear McLaglen's voice shout out, "First team!" That means they're ready to shoot again. I turn and start toward the door. I want to get out before the red light goes on. Out of the corner of my eye I see Rodriguez waving to me and when I catch his eye he points to outside. I nod and duck out just as the bell rings and the light goes on.

Four minutes later Rodriguez emerges from the sound stage and lights up a cigarette as he walks over to me.

"Anything?" I ask.

"Nothing," he says. "I hear you talked with Phoebe Sweets."

"You haven't?"

"Aside from a phone call, no. She's on my list. What's she have to say for herself?"

"You know about Wyckham moving out on her the day before he disappeared."

Rodriguez nods.

"We're trying to run that down and getting no place. Anything else?"

I tell him about Wyckham's change of appearance. He's not surprised. If you're going to pretend to be someone else it helps if you can make yourself look like him. He IS surprised when I tell him about Wyckham's sudden influx of money.

"I checked with payroll," I say. "They never advanced him a dime. Maybe he robbed a bank."

"I'd bet not," Rodriguez says. "Bank robbery is for dummies. This guy is slick and he plans ahead. Ten to one when he moved out he already had new digs arranged for. Since he didn't take Phoebe's car, he was either picked up by a friend or he took a cab which is why we're canvassing all the cab companies looking for the driver who picked him up at Phoebe's address."

"Which should lead you to his new address."

"I sure hope so."

"And if you find him at his new address, you find out where all this money came from."

"That's the plan," Rodriguez says.

"And what would you guess is the source of this sudden wealth?"

"A rich uncle, the Irish Sweepstakes, a printing press, a long shot at the racetrack, a back alley mugging, or some sort of extortion."

"I like that last one," I say.

"So do I," Rodriguez says. "It's a tried and true method with only one real drawback."

"It can get you killed," I say.

"Exactly."

"So you think—?"

"I don't know what I think, Joe," Rodriguez replies. "All I know is, this guy who pretends to be Wyckham is gone and I can't find him and no matter how you look at it, that is not good."

I can find no flaw in his logic.

Back at my office I find two phone slips on my desk. One says 'New York Times" along with a phone number. The other merely says Jimmy Fidler. I'm no fool. The Times gets first call. The young lady on the other end of the line is pleasant and knowledgeable. Three months ago Warners released another movie based on one of Ernie Gann's novels. 'Island in the Sky' was produced by Wayne-Fellows, directed by William Wellman, distributed by Warner Brothers, starred John Wayne and was about a downed airplane in the frozen north. The young lady, whose name is Renee Fitzgibbon, wonders if Mr. Gann would be interested in participating in a major article for the Sunday magazine section, talking about the two books, comparing them and recounting his involvement in the process of bringing the two books to the screen. I take a healthy pause so that I don't blurt out my excitement. Most of the time we feather merchants sweat blood trying to get noticed. Suddenly a major coup has fallen into my lap. Jack Warner will think I am a genius. I will not dissuade him. I tell Renee that she is a bright young lady who knows her stuff and I'm sure if I approach Mr. Gann in the right way, I can get him to agree. This is the same skillful use of persuasion I employ when I try to get a 300 pound dessert freak to participate in a pie eating contest.

I say goodbye to Renee, promising to get back to her, and then I have Glenda Mae get me Jimmy Fidler. Fidler has a nationally syndicated radio show and his audience outstrips Hedda and Louella combined. He has a natural distrust of studio spokesmen (that's me) and the level of animosity is mutual.

"What's going on with the airplane picture?" Fidler growls when his secretary finally puts him on the phone. While waiting I've had Glenda Mae pour me a cup of her delicious chickory-laced coffee, checked out 'Terry and the Pirates' and 'Mary Worth' and filled in half of the daily crossword puzzle.

"What about it, Jimmy?" I ask, feigning ignorance.

"Don't give me that. I hear you've got a missing actor."

Rule Number One. Never lie. Fudge and weasel and skirt the truth but no outright lies. If you lose your credibility, you lose your job.

"As far as I know, everybody is on the set who's supposed to be there," I say.

"And I hear that this guy Wyckham isn't really Wyckham at all," Fidler goes on.

Uh-oh. He's got a pipeline into the studio. Time to watch my step.

"Who told you that?" I ask.

"A reliable source," he says, "and I ask the questions, Joe. Not you. Well?"

"We were forced to replace a bit player named Wyckham who failed to come back from lunch hour last Monday. We believe it might have been a possible family emergency and we are still trying to locate him." I'm very proud of the way I was able to weave "we believe", "might have been" and "possible" into one long non-responsive reply. Fidler is not so easily taken in.

"Cut the crap, Joe. I hear the guy's a ringer and wanted by the cops in two states."

"Untrue," I say adamantly which I can do because Fidler added that last part about the police.

"Okay," he says, "but if I find out you've been yanking my chain—"

"I'm not," I say.

"Better not be," he says and hangs up.

Now I'm in it up to my adams apple. A half-baked rumor with a little bit of truth and a whole lot of hyperbole is a publicity man's worst nightmare. Fidler may run it unverified which will suddenly put the jackals on the scent led by Hedda closely followed by Sheila. Once they get involved no explanation will be good enough, not even the truth which more often than not makes for lousy copy.

And even if Fidler tries to keep it to himself until he can get corroboration, it will leak out. It always does.

I sit back in my chair and stare at the phone. What I need right now, besides a really stiff drink, is another phone call like the one I just got from Renee Fitzgibbon.

Fat chance.

CHAPTER SEVEN

I'm in the office early Thursday morning. even ahead of Glenda Mae. I check the call sheet and see that Bob Stack isn't due on the set until 3:00 this afternoon. I call his home and his housekeeper tells me he is at the range shooting. Stack is a world champion skeet shooter and a regular contributor to gun-themed magazines. She promises to have Stack call me as soon as he returns home. I don't have any better luck with Ernie Gann who sailed to Catalina yesterday aboard his yacht. He's due back late this afternoon. Again I leave word.

My dinner with Senator Knowland last night was a huge success. I dragged along Dexter when I realized that both he and Knowland were graduates of UC Berkeley. What I didn't know and would soon find out was that both were also members of the Zeta Psi fraternity. Knowland is pleased. He's even more pleased when I hand him a sheet of paper with three names on it and next to each name a dollar amount that runs to six figures. He is so delighted he orders the most expensive champagne from the wine list to toast his good fortune. For a moment Dexter thinks his fraternity brother is a real sport. I disillusion him when I pick up the tab at dinner's end. Later I will explain to my young friend the workings of a democratic republic. Politicians never pay for anything. Ever. In their eyes we're damned lucky to have their company. No matter. Warner won't care about the tab and I couldn't be happier. Dexter has just become our official conduit to the Senator which means I'm going to get more nights off.

The phone rings. Since Glenda Mae isn't in yet, I pick up.

"Bernardi."

"Write down this address." I recognize the voice. It's Pete Rodriguez. I grab a slip of paper and write down an address in West Hollywood.

"Done," I say.

"Are you busy?"

"Not yet."

"Drive on over."

"You found Wyckham," I say.

"Could be," he replies.

I find the address near the corner of Highland and Santa Monica. It's a rundown apartment house with a cracked cement sidewalk and dandelions for a lawn. An unmarked black Ford with black wall tires and a whip antenna is parked at curbside. This tells me that Rodriguez is inside.

I go in to find a tiny foyer with tenants' mailboxes lining one wall. The cop watching the staircase gives me the fisheye until I tell him my name. He tells me 2G, up the stairs turn left, end of the hallway. I hurry up the steps. This place is a real rattrap. The dirt on the ceiling is left over from the Hoover adminstration and the smells remind me of a gymnasium locker room. Mr. Big Shot with his flashy wad of greenbacks is obviously not wasting any money on high rent accomodations.

When I enter the room I spot Rodriguez standing in the open door to the bathroom. There's a techie dusting for prints on the dresser that stands against the far wall. A suitcase lies open in the bed. It's been emptied and it's contents carefully laid out for inspection. Standing by the window is a squat bald man in a dirty undershirt and dirtier workpants. He's chewing on an unlit cigar and observing the goings-on with deep suspicion. I take a wild guess that this is the building manager.

Rodriguez waves me over to the bathroom door. Lined up next to the sink are toiletries as well as a bottle of peroxide.

"We got a lucky hit with the cab driver," Rodriguez says. "He picked up our phony Wyckham at Sweets' bungalow in Venice shortly before midnight on Sunday. I showed him the guy's 8x10 glossy and he fingered him. Same for the super. Wyckham rented the place a week ago using the name Johnson and moved a few things in but never slept over until Sunday. He took off early Monday morning and hasn't been back since."

"Not good," I say.

"Not good for Johnson," Rodriquez says."We can't keep the place under surveillance around the clock but I have this creepy feeling it won't make any difference. My gut tells me we've seen the last of our boy. Alive, that is."

I nod.

"Which brings me to you, Joe."

"Me?"

"You told me you didn't know this guy except as Wyckham and even at that, you'd never actually talked to the man."

"That's right," I say.

"Then maybe you can explain this," Rodriguez says as he walks over to the bed. He reaches under a pile of shirts and comes up with a hardcover book. At first I don't recognize it until Rodriguez hands it to me. It's my book, "A Family of Strangers", my one and only novel which sold less than a thousand copies.

Still, it seems unfamiliar until I open it up and discover that it is the version published in Great Britain. Then I notice the personalized inscription. "To Ivor, A thoughtful and generous fan" and it's signed by me.

"Who's Ivor?" Rodriguez asks.

"Damned if I know," I say.

"You signed his book."

I shrug.

"I signed a lot of books." I pause. "Well, maybe not a lot. Some. Hard to remember. I did at least a dozen book signings here in California."

"Not this copy," Rodriguez says and of course he's right. But I was never in the British Isles after the book was published so where did this come from? And even as I ask it of myself, I remember. It was about six months after the book was released and was already on it's way to the remainder market when the package came to the studio. The note was carefully written and very complimentary. I can't remember what it said but it sure bolstered my spirits. The writer wanted me to sign his copy and then send it back to him. He even provided the envelope and the postage.

I tell all this to Rodriguez who listens intently.

"Ivor who?" he asks.

"No clue. It was about three years ago. I remember one thing. It was a Manchester address but aside from that, I've got nothing."

"Maybe that's why he called you at your office. Still a fan. A chance to meet the man who wrote the book in person."

"Maybe so," I say.

"Hey, Pete, I'm done here." the print techie says.

"Okay, we'll clean up and put everything back the way we found it, just in case." He walks over to the super. "Mr. Novak, if your tenant shows, we were never here, you understand?"

The super nods.

"Sure, I get you."

Rodriguez hands him his card. "And if he does show, you call me at this number. Any time of the day."

"No problem," he says, taking the card.

A few minutes later Rodriguez and I are emerging from the apartment house and heading for our cars. Traffic on the street is heavy because of the post office situated across the street. People are entering the building in a steady stream carrying armfuls of brown wrapped packages to be delivered before Christmas. I see that I am partially blocked in by some inconsiderate brain-dead idiot who has double-parked next to me.

"Cite that guy, will you, Pete?" I say.

He shrugs.

"Not my department," he says. "Look, if you remember anything more about your pal Ivor, give me a buzz."

"I'm going to check with my secretary. She remembers everything right down to what tie I wore with what suit on what day."

Rodriguez nods and walks to his car which is NOT hemmed in proving to me that even the dumbest among us can recognize an unmarked police car when they see one. Meanwhile I fume. All I can do is wait but when this sorry excuse for a human being does show up, he's going to be on the receiving end of one really loud verbal ass kicking.

At that moment I look across the street as an elderly lady emerges from the post office with the aid of a cane and starts to cross the street. She is moving so slowly that traffic is starting to back up and horns are being blared by the drivers in the back of the pack. Instinctively I move quickly to help her. She smiles up at me.

"Thank you, young man," she says. "You are very kind."

I try to steer her toward the sidewalk but she veers off toward the car that has me shut in.

"Is this your car?" I ask her with a frown.

"Oh, yes. I feel so badly about having to park in the street like this but with my artificial hip I just can't park blocks away and of course, a long walk like that aggravates my asthma something terrible."

"I'm sure it does," I say, opening the driver's side door for her and helping her behind the wheel.

"I get out so seldom these days, " she says sadly, "but if my grandchildren didn't get their Christmas gifts from Nanny, their little hearts would be broken."

"Well, we can't have that," I say, closing the door for her.

"I hope it's not like this at the Motor Vehicle Bureau this afternoon. I have to get my license renewed. It's been so very long, you know. Almost twelve years." She smiles. "Well, thank you again, young man, and you have a very Merry Christmas."

"And the same to you, ma'am," I say with a smile. I step back as she puts the car in gear and shoots forward, weaving only slightly from side to side, and missing a parked pickup truck by a matter of inches.

Ed Lowery, the FBI agent who I have talked to on the phone but haven't yet met, is waiting for me in my office. We are on a first name basis and he is about what I had expected. Slightly under six feet, he's stocky with thick sandy hair and a ruddy complexion. His grip is firm as he introduces himself and apologizes for barging in without an appointment but there's someone who very much wants to meet me without delay. I am confused as I look around my office but just then a newcomer emerges from my private bathroom, wringing his still damp hands.

"You seem to be missing a hand towel, Mr. Bernardi," he says in an accent that can only be acquired at Eton, "so I won't shake your hand and get us both wet. Neville Waite of Her Majesty's counterintelligence service."

"How do you do," I say.

"I do very well, sir, having received from agent Lowery the package of information which you were good enough to send over to him several days ago."

Waite is probably in his mid-50s, tall and slender, reminiscent of Basil Rathbone, and is immaculately dressed in an expensive lightweight grey flannel suit that shrieks Saville Row. His tie is conservative navy blue with a subtle stripe. His oxfords are highly polished. His cufflinks are modest but almost certainly gold. His show handkerchief in his breast pocket matches his tie. The only thing missing is the black homburg. As if his wardrobe didn't already say it all, his stiff ramrod posture completes the picture. A stoic patriotic Englishman is on the job. Sense of humor not required.

I'm about to invite Waite to sit down but he beats me to it without invitation. I gesture to Lowery who takes the other chair and I go behind my desk and sit.

"So, what can I do for you gentlemen?" I ask.

"You can tell us what you know about Ivor Willoughby." Waite says.

I grin broadly.

"Willoughby!" I say. "Yes, now I remember. Ivor Willoughby, of course."

"Of course what, Mr. Bernardi?" Waite asks stiffly.

I explain to him about the book and the long distance signing by mail.

"Then you didn't know the man."

"No."

"Never met him?"

I shake my head.

"No, never met him."

"What did you do during the war, Mr. Bernardi?"

Antenna up. Cop alert. No matter what their title they're all cops and this guy is fishing for something.

"What's that got to do with anything?" I ask.

"Just answer the question, Mr. Bernardi," Waite says.

"Answer mine first," I say.

Ed Lowery jumps in.

"Aaron warned me there was a little of the wise guy in you, Joe, but this is not the time. We're dead serious here."

I look at him and then nod. Okay, I'll play along.

"I signed up for the Army right after Pearl Harbor, spent ten weeks in basic training where I proved I wasn't good for anything except providing target practice for the Jerries. They took away my rifle, handed me a typewriter and turned me into an information specialist. In late-'43 I got shipped to England and posted to 'Stars and Stripes' where I stayed until after the war."

"Did you cross the Channel?" Waite asks.

"Four days after D-Day. I spent the next ten months chasing Patton and Bradley across France into Germany. When V-E Day hit I was in Bonn but somehow the brass neglected to send me home until November. To this day I still can't look at wiener-schnitzel without getting nauseous."

"And in all that time, you never met or had any dealings with Ivor Willoughby."

"I believe I already answered that."

"For the record."

"For the record, I did not."

"Are you quite sure?" Waite asks.

I look at him with undisguised annoyance. Two can play at

this game.

"Isn't it true, Mr. Waite, that in late 1942 you were able to infiltrate the highest levels of Luftwaffe command and obtain Goering's secret plans for the bombing of Wales?"

"I beg your pardon," he says gruffly.

"No need to beg, sir. Just answer the question."

"Don't be absurd."

"A simple yes or no will do, sir." I say.

"You are wasting my time," Waite says.

I lean forward on my desk and stare him down.

"No, you're wasting mine, Mr. Waite. In a courtroom we call it 'asked and answered'. Now if you have a point to make, get to it or get out."

"There's no need for that, Joe," Lowery says.

"I think there is, Ed. I'm willing to cooperate. I'm not willng to be pushed around by some one time military brass hat, now a mid-level spook, who has mistaken me for his batman."

All the while I have not lost eye contact with Waite and a tense silence fills the room. Finally Waite nods.

"Just so, Mr. Bernardi. You are absolutely right and I apologize. I am, as you say, a one time military officer, Lieutenant Colonel to be precise, and the habits of a lifetime are hard to break. Do forgive me."

"Done," I say with a shrug.

"The reason I am so tenacious is due to the serious nature of my appearance here. I did not travel all the way to your city on a lark. My mission involves the safety and well being of your country, sir, and perhaps mine as well."

"Meaning?"

"Meaning that there is every reason to believe that Ivor Willoughby is an agent for the Soviet Union."

CHAPTER EIGHT

For the next half hour, Neville Waite recounts the saga of Ivor Willoughby. It's actually an intriguing story but Waite manages to reduce it to an arid recitation. Despite him, I find myself captivated by the adventures of that colorless little man who sat so quietly in seat 24A, minding his own business, a faceless nonentity.

He was born and raised in Beeston where his father bred and trained thoroughbreds for the wealthy landowners of the region. The farm was large enough to stable forty horses and they also kept stalls at the nearby race course in Nottingham. Young Willoughby didn't get much in the way of formal education but he learned a great deal about the care and training of thoroughbreds for whom he had no great love. At the age of fifteen he took one of the mares out for a ride and never came back. He wound up in Manchester where he sold the horse and got himself a job as an apprentice to a bookbinder. It was over the next several years that he developed a deep rooted love of books and literature, confiscating imperfect editions not fit to sell at retail and often reading long hours into the night, sopping up the education he'd never had as a youngster in Beeston. At the same time he spent much of the money he'd made from the horse sale to buy flying lessons at a nearby aerodrome. After a month he was flying solo and after six months, he was giving lessons, not buying them. Unwilling to give up his beloved books, he juggled both jobs for the next several months. Then came September of 1939 and his country called upon him to protect its shores from German invasion and he enlisted in the RAF.

Despite the odds against him, he survived the Battle of Britain and two years later he found himself flying fighter escort for the Wellingtons that were pounding away at industrial targets in France and later in Germany. In April of 1943 his luck ran out and his plane went down over the mountainous region near Dijon. He managed to belly land in an open field and immediately scrambled from the plane and headed for the high country nearby, escaping detection from the round the clock German patrols sent out every night for a week.

Eventually he was taken in by a farmer woman named Blanche Duvalier and was able to hide out there for over a month before deciding to make a try for the Channel and England. Again, his luck ran out and he was captured by the Gestapo at the railway station in Tours. They held him for several days, administering the usual torture, and then shipped him off to Colditz Castle, a prisoner of war facility for British, and later American, officers. According to other prisoners he was well liked and trusted and involved in several escape attempts, four of which were successful. He was scheduled to escape himself in a major effort in January of 1945 that involved 36 men but the plan failed because the guards had been tipped off. The Gestapo was brought in to investigate and 8 of the ringleaders were summarily executed. In May the prison was liberated by the Americans but because the castle was located in what was to become walled-off East Germany the Russians took control of the castle before anyone could be repatriated.

Up to this point, Waite explained, everything was verifiable but following the Russian takeover, the situation became muddy. The Russians were in no great hurry to send anyone back home and all officers were closely questioned about their political views. Willoughby might have been one of those who stayed behind, voluntarily or otherwise, or he actually might have escaped. It was reported, though unconfirmed, that he made his way back to the farmhouse in Dijon where he set up housekeeping with Blanche Duvalier who believed she was a war widow. Not so. Apparently her "dead" husband showed up in early 1948 and Willoughby quickly took his leave. In any event, wherever he was and whatever he was doing, there is a lengthy and questionable gap in his life story from May of 1945 until November of 1948 when he presented himself to military authorities in London.

At this point, I halt the proceedings. I need to stretch my legs so I offer my guests refreshments. Coffee or soda or if they wish, something stronger. I opt for coffee, Ed Lowery chooses a Coca-Cola and Waite asks about the choices involving something stronger. When I mention Bushmills Irish Whiskey he raises his hand to stop me from further recitation. Three fingers, no ice, will do nicely, he tells me.

When we are once again settled down, Waite continues.

Willoughby was billeted in a nearby BOQ and questioned intensely for two days about his activities following liberation. He seemed more interested in talking about the failed escape attempt which he laid at the feet of a flying officer named Henry Smythe-James who, he was convinced, was either a traitor or a German plant. RAF records showed no officer by the name of Henry Smythe-James and the file indicates the interrogating officer lent little weight to Willoughby's allegations and said as much. On the third day, Willoughby failed to show up for further questioning and that was the last anyone ever saw of him.

"Until now," I say.

"Until now," Waite agrees.

"I can tell you one place he was in late 1950 or early 1951," I say. "His request that I sign his copy of my novel was mailed from Manchester." Waite takes out a small note pad and jots something down. "And I can tell you something else. During that time period Wylie Wyckham was in Manchester as the managing director of a semi-professional theater group."

"And you know this how?" Waite asks.

"His agent Miss Haworth has a friend in London who has supplied her with a complete rundown of Wyckham's activities up until the day of his death."

"So Willoughby knew Wyckham in Manchester," Waite says.

"Even more likely, Willoughby might have been a part of the theater group," I say.

Waite nods.

"And when Wyckham dies, Willoughby sees his chance to flee England for the United States using Wyckham's personna with which he is totally familiar. Yes, it could have happened that way."

I lean back in my chair toughtfully.

"And then—" I pause. "Let me get this straight. This alleged Soviet spy lives hand to mouth here in America until he meets a gullible young lady who takes him into her home in the name of love and basically supports him for months on end. Sorry, Mr. Waite, but I thought the Russkies treated their spies a little better than that."

"Let's not get ahead of ourselves, Mr. Bernardi. First things first," he says as he rises from his chair. Lowery follows suit. "I'm going to need to speak with this Miss Sweets and also with Detective Rodriguez as soon as possible."

"I can arrange that," Lowery says.

"Excellent," Waite says. "Putting aside the possibility that Willoughby's disappearance was forced upon him, he has gone into hiding for reasons known only to him. My feeling is that we have no time to spare if we are to catch up with him."

I come around my desk. He extends his hand and we shake.

"Sorry we got off to a bad start, Mr. Bernardi," Waite says. "It shan't happen again."

I nod.

"Just one question, Mr. Waite," I say, "'"and its probably silly of me to ask it but in the event that we do stumble across Willoughby, what do you intend to do about him?"

"Return with him to England, naturally," he says.

"I see. And does that mean that you have brought a fugitive warrant with you?"

He smiles.

"The legalities are really not your problem, Mr. Bernardi," he says.

"I only ask because nowhere did you mention that Willoughby was actually wanted officially by your government."

His smile turns icy.

"And here we were starting to get along so well. Pity. Goodbye, Mr. Bernardi."

He turns on his heel and goes out. Lowery throws me a helpless look of commiseration and follows him.

I suppose I should be grateful. With MI6 and the FBI and Pete Rodriguez on the case, my services are definitely no longer needed. I should be breathing a sigh of relief but I'm not. I have a sinking feeling I am not yet done with this puppy.

Glenda Mae hands me two phone slips. Both Bob Stack and Ernie Gann have returned my phone calls. I call Ernie first. He's the easy one. I tell him about Renee Fitzgibbon's idea for a Times feature and I can hear him salivating on the other end of the line. I give him Renee's phone number and tell him to work it out.

Stack is a different story. When he hears what I have in mind he's all in favor of it but I am going to have to sit down and chat with him at length to get a feel for the kind of questions I should be asking him. He's free tomorrow until two o'clock so we set a date for ten a. m. in my office.

When I hang up, I ask Glenda Mae to get me my guy at Photoplay and as I wait for him to come on line I wonder what it will take to get this cover story. 50 yard line seats for the play-offs should the Rams get in? A weekend get away for him and his wife at a seaside resort? A weekend get away for him and Marilyn at a seaside resort that his wife doesn't know about?

At times like these I cringe a little and telling myself that this is the way the game is played is no consolation. I think I'm getting a little jaded. Maybe it's time to turn my attention back to that second novel I have started, the pitifully few pages of which are stacked neatly in my lower desk drawer.

It's never good news when my phone starts jangling in the middle of the night and tonight is no exception. Dog tired I went to bed at 10:30 and actually dropped off immediately but now I am awake and the clock on my night stand reads 1:34. I stumble out of bed and grope my way into the kitchen where my one and only phone unit hangs on the wall.

"Speak," I say gruffly into the mouthpiece.

"Joe, it's Pete Rodriguez,"

Now I know it's trouble.

"What happened?"

"Phoebe Sweets. She's in a bad way. Somebody broke into her bungalow and beat the crap out of her."

"Willoughby?"

"She says no. She's here in Emergency at Brotman in Culver City and she's asking for you."

"I'm on my way," I say and hang up.

I throw clothes on and thirty fve minutes later I'm wheeling into the emergency parking lot of Brotman Medical Center. I hurry inside. Rodriguez sees me and waves me over.

"How is she?" I ask.

"No worse," Rodriguez says. "She's going to hurt a lot for a while but she's in no danger. The son of a bitch used her for a punching bag. Kept asking where it was. Some kind of envelope. She didn't know what he was talking about. Finally he tied her up and gagged her and tore her place apart trying to find it."

"Description?"

Rodriguez smiles humorlessly.

"Sure. Black and red, wool knit, two eyeholes."

"Ski mask."

Rodriguez nods.

"Joe, she asked me what happened to the extra security. I didn't know what she was talking about. She said to ask you."

Suddenly I feel ill. I'd promised to talk to Pete about extra patrols outside her house and in the pressure and confusion of events I forgot all about it. I explain this to Pete. He tells me not to worry about it. Occasional patrols aren't much of a deterent.

I ask if I can see her and he leads me in to a cubicle along one wall of the emergency room. She's awake and in obvious pain but she smiles when she sees me and reaches out for my hand. Her head is swathed with bandages and one eye is badly swollen.

Her jaw is badly bruised and there are abrasions on her cheeks.

"You were right," she says with a wan smile, holding my hand.

"I wish I hadn't been," I say.

"Guess I look a mess."

"Nothing that won't clear up in a week."

"Even my ribs?"

"Oh, In that case, maybe two weeks," I say. "Look, Phoebe, I am so sorry. I forgot to talk to Detective Rodriguez about those extra patrols."

"Forget about it," she says. "He came in the back way. Chances are they'd never have spotted him."

"What can you tell me about him? Anything?"

"Not really. He was tall. About your height, Joe. And he was white. He spoke well. No accent or anything like that."

"Clothes?"

"Dark colors. Blue jeans, I think. A windbreaker. Dark blue." She pauses. "One thing. A little strange. He didn't wear a wrist watch but he did wear a plain copper bracelet on one of his wrists."

"Some people think it relieves the pain of arthritis."

She shakes her head.

"If he had arthritis, he sure didn't show it. And who walks around these days without a wrist watch? Weird."

I smile and squeeze her hand, promising to find the guy who did this to her.

"Don't worry about it, Joe," she says.

"But I do worry about it, Phoebe," I say.

I lean down and kiss her forehead and tell her to try to get some sleep and then I walk out into the reception area.

"Anything?" Rodriguez asks.

"Only that it wasn't Willoughby."

"And if not Willoughby, then who?" Rodriguez asks.

"Why, the guy he was blackmailing, of course," I say. "It's probable there's something incriminating floating around somewhere and this guy's not going to rest until he finds it."

"You're guessing."

"It's more than a guess and you know it. Willoughby comes into sudden money, rents an apartment but doesn't move in, gets abducted from the studio lot and taken God knows where. Is he still alive? Maybe, maybe not. Has he been beaten to obtain this piece of incriminating evidence? Probably. Has his victim found it yet? Who knows? It wasn't at the new apartment because you searched it thoroughly. If it was in Phoebe's bungalow he probably has it by now but if he doesn"t, this guy is liable to get very desperate and by me, very desperate means very dangerous."

Rodriguez scratches his head.

"I'm trying to remember how I got mixed up in this thing?"

"Just plain lucky, Pete. Have you met Lt. Colonel Neville Waite yet?' I ask.

"Pip pip," he grins. "Us Colonials are so blessed to have him helping out."

"I knew you'd be appreciative." I check my watch. "Time to hit the sack again. If I'm lucky I'll get four or five hours sleep before duty calls." I salute him goodbye and head for the door.

On the drive back to the Valley my mind is a jumble of thoughts. Is Ivor Willoughby a Russian agent? I seriously doubt it. I wonder if Waite doubts it, too, or if he's just following orders. Last year I spent a couple of weeks filling in on a Cornel Wilde WWII picture about traitors and double agents. The technical advisor was a former British commando officer named Brixton, a friendly outgoing guy not at all like Waite. One night we were sitting around a bar and I asked him how things really worked in MI6 and the CIA. When he was positive I really wanted to know and wasn't afraid of the answer, he pulled his chair closer and told me. Warrants and extradition papers are nice to bandy about and they give great comfort to the lily-livered idealists among us but they have nothing to do with the real process of dispensing justice. More wrongs have been righted with the business end of a Walther PPk than any panel of twelve men good and true. Does this sound like retired Lt. Colonel Neville Waite, now of her Majesty's counterintelligence service? You bet your ass it does and I fear for Ivor Willoughby if Waite catches up with him before Ed Lowery or Pete Rodriguez.

CHAPTER NINE

It takes a lot to quell Glenda Mae's natural exuberance and I really never thought I'd see the day when she'd be cowed into awe struck adoration but the day has arrived. At 9:33 I walk into my office and there's the Duke, sitting on the edge of Glenda Mae's desk, smiling down at her as they chat, and there's Glenda Mae. staring up at him with Betty Boop eyes and a mouth that is almost agape.

Wayne smiles in greeting.

"Joe, why didn't you tell me about this little lady you've got stashed up here?"

"Does the mouse tell the cat where he keeps his cheese?" I say.

Wayne pretends to be hurt.

"Are you intimating that I would try to steal this lovely young thing away from you?"

"The minute my back was turned, Duke," I say.

"Well, if that don't beat all," he mutters. He takes Glenda Mae's hand. "You remember what I told you, Missy. The moment this fella steps out of line, you come and see me."

"I will, Mr. Wayne," she stutters.

"And that's Duke. Don't forget it."

"I won't," she says.

Wayne lifts himself off the desk, crushing out the cigarette he's been smoking, and throws a massive arm around my shoulders. He leads me to my office.

"Come on, Joe. You and me have some talking to do."

We go in and Wayne closes the door, then turns to me. The smile has disappeared from his face.

"Okay, Joe," he says, "what's this about us having a Commie on our set?"

"Where'd you hear that, Duke?"

"Aw, knock it off. It's all over the studio. Now stop pussyfootin' around and give it to me straight."

"First of all it may not even be true."

"Not the way I heard it," Wayne says. He reaches in his shirt pocket for his pack of Camels and lights up with a battered Zippo displaying the USMC logo.

"An agent from Britain's MI6 got here yesterday—" I start to say.

"I've met him. Kind of opinionated."

"Doesn't mean he's right."

"Doesn't mean he's wrong. I'm going to assume the studio is cooperating in trying to find this guy Wyckham, Willoughby, or whatever the hell his name is."

"We are. LAPD and the FBI are also in on it."

Wayne shakes his head annoyed.

"How's something like this happen, Joe?"

"Fake passport, fake visa, fake resume."

"Well, it's not going to happen, Joe. Not on one of my pictures. We fought a war to wipe out the Nazis and we'll fight another one if we have to to get rid of these Commie sons of bitches."

"Let's hope it doesn't come to that, Duke."

"Yeah, let's hope. Meanwhile, when you find this guy you make sure he gets shipped back to England by plane, by boat or swimming, I don't much care which, just make sure he's gone."

"I'll do my best."

Wayne's smile comes back. He squashes his cigarette in an ashtray I keep handy for visitors.

"Good man."

He turns and goes to the door and opens it.

"Keep beating the drums for the picture, Joe. We've got a winner here."

I walk him out into the anteroom.

"I don't suppose I could talk you into sitting down for a photo spread for one of the national magazines?"

Wayne laughs.

"Well, there's an idea. You could have some fella follow me and some of the boys around with a camera to a few of our favorite watering holes and watch us get happy. Very, very happy. You might say I lead an interesting life, Joe, but not one you'd want to cover in a family magazine."

And of course, I realize he's right. I've heard the rumors of his affairs with several exceptionally willing ladies notably Marlene Deitrich. And his drinking habits are legendary. It's common knowledge when the booze gets out of hand he becomes a hard man to live and work with. Still, I'm not ready to give up.

"How about Duke Wayne at home with wife and kids? How many are still in the nest? Three?"

"Last time I looked which was a while ago. Don't spend much time at the homestead these days, Joe. Not with Esperanza threatening to shoot me if I walk in the door. She tried once, you know. Almost got me."

"I didn't know she was still at it," I say.

"I don't advertise it," he says. "My lawyer's talking to her lawyer. This time next year things'll be different but for now, the Wayne family home life is nobody's business but our own." He takes out the pack of Camels and again lights up.

"It'll stay that way," I say.

"Good man," he says. He looks past me at Glenda Mae and smiles. "Nice meeting you, Missy. You take care now," he says.

"I will, sir," Glenda Mae croaks as Wayne opens the door, ducks his head and goes out.

I look at Glenda Mae who is still staring at the door. I consider asking her to get me a cup of coffee but immediately realize she is going to be useless for the rest of the morning. I check my watch. Too late for coffee, anyway. I'm due at Bob Stack's dressing room in six minutes. I tell Glenda Mae where I'll be. She fails to respond. I leave. I tell myself she'll be her old self by lunch time. I sure hope so.

Wayne is one thing. Bob Stack's another. While the Duke is bigger than life and known throughout the world, Stack is quiet, introspective and little known outside of the Hollywood community. But that doesn't mean he is dull because he isn't. He is a man of eclectic tastes, a world class sportsman who excels at skeet, a champion caliber polo player and a renowned outboard motorboat racer. He's probably best known to the public as the man who gave Deanna Durbin her first on-screen kiss but that was fifteen years ago and hardly current news. He made something of an impression playing opposite Carole Lombard in "To Be or Not to Be", a Jack Benny vehicle which shed the light of truth on the Nazis while still managing to evoke a few laughs. He took time out to serve in the Navy as a gunnery instructor and when he returned to Hollywood he appeared in a string of forgettable parts in forgettable films. Then last year he starred in

"Bwana Devil", the first movie to be shot in 3D and got a little press out of it which may be one reason why he was tapped to play the pilot in this picture, despite Wellman's friendship with Robert Cummings who was originally slated for the role. Stack realizes, as does his manager Bertha, that this role in this movie could be a career changer and he wants to make the most of it.

After an hour chatting I have enough to put something interesting together. We debate the approach. Sure fire is the "eligible bachelor" angle, always viable with a good looking young leading man like Stack. Just as effective might be "virile leading man" playing opposite John Wayne in a tense action packed thriller. We decide to sleep on it and chat the next morning. Meanwhile I arrange with Buddy Raskin, my pet studio photographer, to get together with Bob and take a few rolls of film at home and on the set and participating in his favorite sports.

Back at the office, things are not quite back to normal. Glenda Mae is on the phone with some of her studio gal-pals telling them about her encounter with the Duke. She gives me a hard look which I translate to mean, 'Don't bother me, I'm busy'. I head into my office to work the phone on my own.

I call the hospital but Phoebe's already been released. I make a note to call her later at home. Pete Rodriguez has nothing new to report except that Neville Waite is making a royal pain in the ass out of himself believing, in his quaint British way, that the local police and the FBI exist to serve at his pleasure. In the spirit of international cooperation he is being momentarily tolerated but Pete assures me it won't last long. Airlines, bus stations and Union Station have all been covered as a matter of protocol but Willoughby could easily have slipped out of the city anytime in the past four days. A BOLO (Be on the Lookout) has been issued for the 11 western states but this, too, is form, not substance. If Willoughby is gone, he's gone and there's little we can do about it.

My phone rings. I wait for Glenda Mae to pick up, then realize that I can wait until sundown and it will still be ringing. I have this perverse urge to rat her out to her husband, Beau, but I know if do, I'll never again taste a decent cup of coffee. I sigh and pick up. Jack Warner's secretary is on the line. He needs to see me immediately. Most urgent. Two of my least favorite words. Immediately and urgent.

"i know it's short notice, Joe, but I need you tomorrow night," Jack says before I've even had a chance to sit down. "I'd handle it myself but I'm taking Jackie down to the Del Coronado in San Diego for the weekend." I don't have to ask who Jackie is. Everyone at the studio knows about her relationship with Jack. It's been going on for several years and it's deep rooted which is why Warner is not about to change his plans but I'm expected to change mine.

But tomorrow? No, no. not tomorrow. Impossible. I am going to have Yvette all to myself for almost 24 hours and more than that, I have given my word to Jillian. This can't be happening. Yet it is and for the second time in three days I am going to have to tell Jack L. Warner that I am not available to do his bidding. He was understanding last time. This time I fear he will construe my reluctance for rebellion.

"The fellow's name is Boulle. French. He's a novelist and he's written this book. WW II stuff about a Japanese prison of war camp in Burma and the Japs have orders to build this railway bridge over this river using prisoners of war."

"Based on a true story?"

"Maybe. The book's fiction although there was such a bridge. Anyway, it sounds like pretty dreary stuff. Prisoners getting whipped and dying of disease and malnutrition. And then this Colonel ends up collaborating with the Japs. Stiff as a pool cue, you know the type, kind of like the MI6 spook that's wandering all over my studio. '

"Yes, I do know the type," I say, thinking Waite sounds like this Colonel's twin brother.

"He's in town for the weekend so take the guy out to some-place nice and see if there's anything there."

"Sounds like something more suited to Hal Wallis or Henry Blanke," I say, referring to Jack's star producers.

"They're tied up," Warner says.

I mention three other lesser Warners contract producers. No go. They are also unavailable. Moment of truth.

"I'm also unavailable, Jack," I say.

He gives me a hard look.

"Didn't we go through this about three days ago?"

"We did and I have to beg off for the same reason," I tell him.

"Does this reason outweigh your continued employment at Warner Brothers Studio?"

"Yes."

Warner hesitates.

"Look, if this is some dame—"

"It isn't."

"You threatened me once, Joe, and I backed away. I can't do it again. "

"Maybe I can get this guy Boulle to meet me earlier on Saturday or even on Sunday."

"Maybe. But he warned me that he and Lean have a lunch date on Sunday at Harry Cohn's house."

"Lean?" I say. "David Lean?"

"Yeah. The guy who does all those Dickens things. I think it's a package deal though what Dickens has got to to with Japs in the jungle is beyond me." He pauses. "So, Joe, what's it going to be?" He stares at me hard,

I hesitate and then I say, "I'll let you decide, Jack."

And then I tell him my story, about Jillian and about Yvette and about a fatherhood that doesn't really exist. When I'm finished, I lean forward in my chair and stare into Warner's eyes.

"Ball's in your court, Jack." I say to him.

He hesitates, regarding me curiously, and then he nods.

"You're a damned fool, Joe. Nothing good can come from your relationship with this woman."

"With all due respect, sir, that's my lookout."

Warner twiddles his fingers for a moment, staring out his window and then he looks back at me.

"Okay, Joe. Call Boulle, try to reschedule. If he can't, send Dexter. If Dexter's not good enough to take the meeting, then the hell with him. Harry Cohn's welcome to him."

I get up from my chair and reach across the desk, hand extended.

"They say you're a big man in this town, Jack. As far as I'm concerned, you're a big man, period." We shake. "I'll keep you posted," I say.

I head for the door and as I reach it I hear Warner call my name. I turn. He's still seated.

"That's twice I've made an accommodation for you, Joe. There won't be a third time. You'd better learn now that unless you are sitting in this chair you have no personal life that isn't superseded by the studio. Twenty four hours a day, seven days a week, you and everyone else around here belongs to me. Those who disagree are free to leave. Much as I like and admire you, Joe, that includes you. Don't put me in this position again."

I nod, humbled.

"I won't, J. L. ," I say.

He nods back and flicks me goodbye with a wave of his hand. I go out.

As I walk into my office I find Glenda Mae on the phone. She looks up and then says,"Wait a minute, Harry. He just walked in the door." She holds out the phone to me. "Harry Davis," she says.

I take it from her.

"Harry, what's up?"I say.

"Got a guy here at the gate claims he has an appointment with you. He's not on the list and your girl never heard of him."

"What's his name?"

"Finch. Alexander Finch. Says he works for the London Daily Mail."

"You check his I. D. ?"

"He looks legit," Harry says. "Wait a minute." I can hear Harry covering the mouthpiece and then muffled voices. Then Harry comes back on the phone. "He says to tell you if you give him twenty minutes, he'll give you the real dope on Neville Waite."

Now that sounds interesting.

"Send him up," I say.

Alexander Finch is a ferret faced little man with long stringy hair that may have been washed last month but it's debatable whether shampoo was involved. His teeth are crooked and tobacco stained and he peers at me over horn rimmed glasses as I inspect the business card which he has handed me. He is identified as a journalist for the London Daily Mail, a reputable newspaper with a storied past. The paper's phone number is listed on the card.

"What happens if I call this number?" I ask.

He shrugs, taking a sip of the tea I have given him.

"I get sacked. Won't be the first time, won't be the last," he says.

"Then I take it you are here on your own farthing, so to speak." I'm working on a mug of Glenda Mae's coffee.

"Right you are," he says. His accent is working class, maybe not cockney but close to it. "The boss thinks I'm on holiday in Scotland."

"But instead you've followed Neville Waite here to Los Angeles."

"Right again, Guv."

"Any particular reason?" I ask.

"I'm a reporter, that's why, and where Waite goes, trouble follows like mud puddles after a rainstorm."

"Do you know why he's here?"

"No, but I will. Maybe you could tell me."

"Maybe I could and maybe I will, but you go first, Mr. Finch. I'll grant you twenty minutes to give me the real dope on Neville Waite."

He nods.

"Maybe you've noticed, he's a bit of a prig."

"I've noticed."

"Don't let that fool you, mate. The man's a stone cold killer with a badge. Got a taste for it during the war, he did, and it's stayed right with him. Now instead of Nazis, it's subversives but he doesn't really care. Enemies are enemies and dead is dead and he prides himself on the amount of money he saves the crown by eliminating the need for trials."

"You're talking murder," I say, leaning back in my chair.

"There's talk he has a by-your-leave from the Crown," Finch says.

"Meaning?"

"Meaning maybe he and couple of others have blanket permission to execute Her Majesty's enemies without the cumbersome meddling of the justice system."

"And you have first hand knowledge of this?"

"Nineteen-fifty-one. I'm tracking down an espionage story involving a university professor named Thimbleford. He's working with a draftsman in one of the aircraft factories shuttling designs and other classified material to the Russians. A real looney. One of those One-Worlders, anti-military, anti-war and anti-Good King George. One day I follow him to a deserted warehouse down by the docks when I run into Waite and three of his goons who have caught up with Thimbleford. I try to get up the stairs to question him but two of the goons grab me and take me out and toss me in the trunk of their car. Three hours later they set me free maybe twenty kilometers outside the city. By the time I get back the story's all over the news. The professor leaped from a window into the Thames in an effort to escape and drowned in the process."

"Could have happened that way," I say.

"That night I get a call from one of my buds who works in the morgue. He tells me Thimbleford has a small caliber bullet hole just behind his right ear. I take it to my editor who tells me to forget it. The guy's dead. Story's over. Move on to something else."

"Your editor caved." I say.

"He had a choice. He could be fired and go on the dole or keep his mouth shut and keep his job."

"Maybe the same thing could happen to you," I suggest.

Finch laughs.

"They don't scare me. In '45 I get mustered out and spent a

year living off the land near the Cotswolds. Two years ago I had a big expose on this crooked real estate mogul. The cops were dragging their feet because somebody was on the pad so I set up a tent in Hyde Park and went on a hunger strike for fifteen days until they finally broke down and did their bloody job. So, am I afraid, Mr. Bernardi? Afraid of what? I say bugger the bunch of them."

In spite of myself I have to laugh. Finch smiles.

"So if I read this right, you keep a steady eye on Waite and when he makes a move, you move with him."

"You've got it. And now maybe you'll tell me what the bastard's doing over here."

I shrug.

'Not my place to reveal that, Mr. Finch, but I will tell you this much. An actor has disappeared from the set of one of our movies and it's possible, though by no means certain, that the man is a Soviet agent. I repeat, possible. We have no proof, only conjecture."

"That won't mean much to Waite," Finch says.

I tell him to interview the police and I give him Pete Rodriguez's phone number. If Pete has no problem with him, he's got himself a story. After a few more minutes he gets up to go. He thanks me for seeing him and tells me he is staying at the Shamrock Motel on Ventura Boulevard in Studio City. I write down the number. After he leaves, I buzz Glenda Mae. She's almost herself again. I give her the number in London and tell her I want to speak to the managing editor. I'm pretty sure Finch is who he says he is but this case is attracting an odd cast of characters and I don't want any unpleasant surprises. She gets some sort of receptionist who says the editor is in a meeting but he'll call back as soon as he's free. Again, the magic of the

Warner Brothers name is at work.

In less than five minutes, the editor's on the phone. He speaks with a wheezy upper class accent and halfheartedly vouches for Finch who matches the description I supply. He's described to me as a 'roman candle' or what some might call a 'loose cannon'. A sharp, inquisitive reporter with no sense of decorum and who, in the editor's opinion, has a deep seated vendetta against MI6 in general and Neville Waite in particular. His advice? Handle with caution. I thank him and hang up. As I do, I look up and Bertha Bowles is standing in my open doorway.

"You look hungry," she says.

I glance at my watch. It's 1:45.

"Matter of fact, I am," I say.

"Let's go," she says. "Art's Deli. I'm buying."

CHAPTER TEN

Art's Deli is a wildly popular noshery for Valleyites and is almost always jammed but at 2:00, the luncheon crowd has thinned out and we have no trouble getting a table. Art himself takes our order. Kreplach soup and a bagel for Bertha, a mile-high turkey, pastrami and swiss on rye for me. To eat the thing you need jaws like a great white shark or a knife and fork or a great deal of optimism. I opt for the latter. It's slow going but the sandwich is delicious.

"Bob says your meeting this morning went very well," Bertha says after we are settled in with our food.

"I thought so. A nice man, Very bright."

"I don't manage losers," Bertha says. "And speaking of losers, how is Jack Warner these days?"

I almost laugh.

"I'd hardly call one of the town's most successful moguls a loser," I say.

"I would," Bertha says. "As an executive, I'd rate him only so-so, more lucky than anything else. As a human being he rates a D-. He escapes an F because I hear he's good to his dog."

"Don't you think you're being a little tough on him. He's always treated me fairly."

"That's because until this year you had Charlie Berger taking the hits. With Charlie gone, you stand naked and unarmed."

"So far I have no problems," I say.

This is not exactly true. I've been chewed out royally on several occasions and Warner's language would make a San Francisco madame blush but bottom line, I'm still in love with my job and for this I can tolerate Jack Warner's petty tyranny.

"Wait," Bertha says in warning, sipping her soup. She dabs at her mouth with her napkin and then starts to slather cream cheese on her bagel. I'm a little confused. She says she ordered the soup to keep her weight down. How the bagel figures into this equation I do not know.

"Charlie's doing well," she says.

"So he tells me."

"We had a long chat on the phone this morning. He thinks the world of you, Joe."

"It's mutual," I say.

"So how long do you think you're going to stick around Warners in the face of everything that's going on."

"And what would that be?" I ask, playing dumb though I have a pretty good idea what she's talking about.

"How many contract players are left at the studio, Joe?" she asks.

"Off hand I couldn't say."

"A lot less than there were eight years ago. Same for MGM, Twentieth, Paramount. The business is changing fast. Very fast and some of the studios are going to be part of it and some are going to be left behind. Look at the picture you're making now. It's not a Warners picture, it's a Wayne-Fellows picture and Jack Warner is supplying a checkbook and distribution but it sure isn't like the old days."

"What's your point, Bertha?"

"My point is, the independents are sprouting up everywhere. Bogart makes pictures for Santana Productions. He owns it. Burt Lancaster's a partner in Hecht-Lancaster. You want Burt, you do business with his company or you don't do business. United Artists is starting to make deals all over town with people like the Mirisch Brothers and Billy Wilder. No studio, no back lot, no huge plant to keep operating, no overhead. How long can Warners and the other dinosaurs keep operating the old way? How long before they start leasing out sound stages and their support facilities? How long before they realize that a publicity department on payroll week after week is something they can no longer afford?"

I lay my half-eaten sandwich down on my plate.

"Thanks for the indigestion," I say.

"Don't whine, Joe. You're no dinosaur and never have been and when it comes to press relations, you're one of the top three in the industry."

I laugh.

"Yeah? And who says that?"

"The people I've been talking to. Important actors and directors, studio executives, Dore Schary, Zanuck."

She looks me in the eye and I look back. She's dead serious.

"What am I doing here, Bertha?" I ask.

"Getting an education and listening to a career opportunity if you're so inclined. My operation is growing fast. Too fast. I need help."

I shake my head.

"I don't know anything about managing talent," I say.

"And I don't know anything about publicity," she says. "I suggest we get married."

I smile, shaking my head.

"And we haven't even had a first date kiss yet."

"We start a new company. Bowles & Bernardi or the other way around, I don't care. I do what I do, you do what you do. I have the contacts and I have the clients and there are more I could sign tomorrow if I had the time and the energy to do them justice. But I don't. And that's why I either stay a little guppy in the fish tank or I bring you on board. If things keep growing, and I'm sure they will, we hire new people. Instead of working for a weekly paycheck, you'll be on your way to becoming a millionaire."

I shake my head again, not negatively, but trying to absorb everything she's said.

"It sounds—" I grope for the right word. "—challenging," I say.

"But?"

"But it's a lot to take in all at once."

"I understand, Joe, and I'm not asking for an answer now or even in the next few days. But sleep on it. Weigh it. You're single. You can afford to take a flyer and I know for sure you don't want to be an also-ran the rest of your life. Is there a risk? Yes, a small one but with your reputation, you'll never have to worry about being out of work. Give this a fair shot. I think you and I could make a hell of a pair."

She smiles and raises her iced tea in a toast and drinks. I follow suit but in truth I don't know whether to be excited, confused or scared to death. Maybe a little of each.

All is quiet when I return to the office. No outstanding phone calls. No threatening letters from collection agencies. On my desk is a slim folder from Dexter dealing with the Eddie Cantor movie. I glance at it. His ideas are no better than mine, just wordier. I shove it aside and ask Glenda Mae to get me Pierre Boulle on the phone. I supply the number and she dials it and a minute or so later I am connected.

"Hello," I say. "M. Boulle?"

"No, my name is Aubert. Who is this?"

"Joseph Bernardi of Warner Brothers Studios. May I speak to M. Boulle?"

"Do you speak French?"

"No, I do not," I say.

"Then you will not be speaking to M. Boulle."

"Strange. I understood that Mr. Warner has a dinner engagement tonight with M. Boulle."

"He does. I am the interpreter."

"Well, Mr. Warner regrets he cannot attend and neither can I."

"You? What have you got to do with this?" Aubert asks.

"Mr. Warner asked me to take the meeting, perhaps earlier in the day."

"Impossible. Without Mr. Warner there is no meeting. Where is he?"

"Out of town on a matter of the most importance."

"And M. Boulle is not?" he says with disdain. "I will convey your regrets." He hangs up and I find myself staring into a dead phone.

This has been going on for nearly eight years now and shows no signs of improving. Something in the drinking water is causing a nationwide outbreak of memory loss among the French people or maybe it's just plain ingratitude. If the boys buried in Flanders Field or at the Omaha cemetery had a vote they'd probably opt for the latter. We saved these ingrates from the Germans in WWI and we did it again in 1944 and I have no idea why we bothered. Their wine is good, their cheeses acceptable but beyond that they have nothing to brag about. I think Jack Warner and I are both well rid of this dinner meeting and Harry Cohn deserves whatever happens to him. If we're lucky the river Kwai will drown the bunch of them.

That's it. I've had enough of the studio for one week. I am going to head for home, change into something comfortable, stretch out on my patio chaise with a cold beer and read a couple of chapters of Ernie Gann's new book 'Soldier of Fortune' before I fall asleep. I give Glenda Mae the rest of the afternoon off and out I go, down the steps to my car. I almost make it. Before I have a chance to slip behind the wheel a gaudy new black Cadillac Fleetwood pulls into the empty spot next to me. I expect a liveried chauffeur to get out but it's only Byron Constable.

"Glad I caught you, Joe," he says. "We need to talk."

"See you Monday," I say forcing a smile.

He pulls out that damned silver pocket watch and checks it out. I know what it says. It's only a minute or two past four.

"I'm sure you still have time to spare me thirty minutes," he says.

"Actually, I don't. Have a nice weekend."

"Excuse me, Bernardi, but I put in my hours around here. I expect you to do the same."

The man really does love the sound of that word "I".

"Expect all you like, Constable, but I don't work for you, and God willing, I never will."

"As a matter of fact, Bernardi, you do work for me. As part of our arrangement with the studio, our use of facilities is itemized for bookkeeping purposes. Publicity is one such facility and I need to talk to you in some detail about our plans for the release of press kits and also the nature and scope of the interviews we'll be scheduling for the supporting players."

I hesitate with my hand on the front door handle.

"Let me ease your mind," I say. "I am perfectly capable of shipping out press kits however and whenever I choose. I will also have no trouble working up all kinds of flattering and informative interviews with our stellar cast of well-known featured actors and actresses. This is what I do, not what you do, though if anyone asked me, I'd be hard pressed to tell them exactly what it is that you do do."

He glares at me. His hatred is right there, just below the surface.

"I can have you fired," he hisses.

"No, you can't but feel free to try. Mr. Warner loves a good joke."

He shrugs sullenly.

"Of course, I will report this incident to Mr. Fellows."

"Thanks," I say graciously. "Saves me the trouble."

He throws me one more dirty look and starts to get back into his car.

"Wait!" I call out, coming around my car to confront him. "I just remembered I had something I wanted to ask you. How come you recommended Wylie Wyckham for the bit part in the picture?"

"I didn't," he says defensively.

"Ah, but you did," I say. "Casting says the pressure came from your office and your boss never heard of the guy."

"You're wrong," Constable says.

"No, I'm not. You are. Have you any idea what a straight answer is? I don't think so. What are you hiding?"

"Nothing."

"Where's Wyckham?" I say.

"You're delusional."

"How about Judge Crater? No, I forgot. You're Canadian. You wouldn't know about him. How about Dr. Livingstone?"

Constable gets in his car without another word, fires it up and backs away. He's insulted, enraged and totally confused. I couldn't ask for more as I watch him race toward the gate shattering the studio speed limit of 5 mph. I truly believe that Mother Nature invents people like Byron Constable to keep the rest of us amused as well as to assure us that no matter how stupid we may feel at any given moment, there is a Byron Constable close by to prove it could be worse.

CHAPTER ELEVEN

It's a toss and turn night, up and out of bed three times, a hot glass of milk, a couple of chapters of Gann's book which does nothing to put me to sleep. Quite the opposite. It spikes my adrenalin. I think I dozed off around three o'clock. Now I hear the phone ring and I'm out of bed instantly and hurry into the kitchen. Too much going on in my life to ignore it. I pray it isn't Jill with a change of plans for tonight. I've been looking forward to my overnight with Yvette all week.

It's pitch dark out as I fumble for the light switch, then glance up at the clock on the kitchen wall. It reads 5:16.

"Hello."

"Mr. Bernardi?"

"Yes."

"Harry Davis, Mr. Bernardi. From the studio."

"What's up, Harry?"

"I hate calling you like this, sir, but Mr. Warner's out of town and he once said to me if there was a problem and he couldn't be reached that I was to call you."

"And is there a problem, Harry?"

"Yes, sir. You might say that. We've found Mr. Wyckham."

I'm dressed and out the door in twelve minutes. I've thrown

on a light windbreaker and I'm immediately sorry I didn't opt for something sturdier. It's bitter cold out and I start to shiver a little even as I get behind the wheel of my car. I start the engine and flip on the heat. It take a while to kick in and I'm halfway to the studio before the interior of the car starts to warm up. Harry's told me to drive directly to the section of the backlot that doubles for New York City and as I approach I can see two studio cruisers parked near some emergency lights which have been set up to illuminate the scene.

I park my car and hurry toward Harry who is standing near a street light. He sees me and hurries in my direction.

"One of my patrols spotted him hanging there about an hour ago," he says.

I look past him and I can see that Wyckham, nee Willougby, has been strung up by his feet from a lamppost and obviously, he is very, very dead.

We walk over to the body.

"Have you called the police?" I ask.

"No, sir. I called you."

I look around. It's me and Harry and three of his security officers and no one else. Harry's good at parking tickets. This one is beyond him. I don't blame him for passing the buck. I check my watch. It's almost six o'clock and still dark and still cold. December's like that, even in sunny California.

"Have one of your men call Van Nuys station and tell them to get Detective Rodriquez over here right away. Tell them we're going to need a coroner's van."

"Right." He waves to one of his men. They confer quietly as I take a closer look at what's left of Ivor Willoughby.

The first thing I notice, and I can hardly avoid it, is the piece of paper on his chest, pinned there by an ugly looking knife driven deep into his chest. Written on the paper in bold block letters is the inscription, " SIC SEMPER PRODITOR".

What's worse is, someone with a sadistic streak has torn him apart from top to bottom. His face is a mass of cuts and bruises and caked blood. One eye looks as if it had been partially gouged out. I kneel down and take a close look at his hands which dangle a foot or so above the street. I know better than to touch the body but I sense both hands have been broken. His fingernails have been pried off and the little finger on one hand has been severed. Whoever did this was a professional when it came to torture and fairly or otherwise, I immediately think of Neville Waite.

When Harry walks back to me, I point to the body and ask, "What's this remind you of?" He shrugs. It doesn't come to him. I help with a hint. "Italy. 1945."

Harry nods. He, too, sees it.

"Mussolini."

"Right," I say.

At the end of April in 1945, Mussolini and his mistress Clara Petacci were trying to flee to Switzerland when they were caught by partisans near Lake Como. They were shot and their bodies transported to Milan where they were hung upside down in a gas station and their corpses vilified by the Italian people for several days. I see a parallel. So does Harry.

I point to the message.

"How's your latin?"

"Lousy," Harry says.

"Mine, too. Where's the nearest outside telephone line?"

Harry thinks for moment and then points to the false front of a movie theater. "Right inside the door to the left."

I nod.

"The commissary should be open by now. Have them send over a couple of gallons of coffee and a couple of dozen danish. It's going to get crowded around here pretty damned fast."

Harry nods as I walk over to the facade of the 'Bijou Theater' and walk through the front doors. To my left is the phone. My first call is to my lawyer, Ray Giordano. No, I don't need a lawyer but Saturday morning is reserved for basketball at the Y. I am one of a dozen or so overweight or out of shape "oldsters" who participate and the only legitimate excuse for missing participation is death. Not death in the family. Your own death. Every other excuse is looked on with a jaundiced eye and total skepticism. Since I have awakened him before seven a. m. he is in a foul mood to begin with it. It gets fouler when I tell him I will not be joining the gang for this morning's festivities. He will be forced to play Porky Horschock in my stead. Porky gets winded at the tip off, has no shot and can't play defense. Ray is not happy. I hang up, even as Ray continues to rant at me, and pull a card out of my wallet. I dial the number. It rings nine times before it's picked up.

"This had better be good," comes the grumbling voice that belongs to my cop buddy, Aaron Kleinschmidt.

"Who's got Josh this weekend? You or the missus?"

"Bernardi, what the hell is this, twenty questions? Do you know what time it is?"

"Who's got the kid?" I repeat.

"She does."

"Good. Come to the studio. I have a surprise for you."

"If it's a dead body, Joe, it's no surprise."

"Maybe not but you're going to love this one."

"This is my day off."

"You don't have days off, Aaron. You have work days and

you have days that you wish were work days. Come on over, Aaron. I need you. I want someone working this case that I can talk to."

"Not interested."

"The victim's a refugee from England, maybe a Communist agent, using another man's identity. He disappeared from the set five days ago under mysterious circumstances. British intelligence arrived Thursday looking for him and now we just discovered his corpse, brutally tortured and strung up from a lamp post like Mussolini when the partisans found him trying to flee the country in 1945."

There is a long silence.

"I'll be there in thirty minutes," he says.

"Bring your team," I say. "We're going to need everybody."

I hang up.

I was right about one thing. It got crowded really fast. It's now eight o'clock. The sun's rising in the east and the emergency lights are no longer needed. Aaron's questioning Harry Davis while his forensic team is busy gathering evidence, trying to get prints from what's left of Willoughby's fingers. Meanwhile the official police photographer is snapping photos from every angle. Pete Rodriguez is nearby questioning the security guard covering the front gate to find out who entered the studio grounds from six the previous evening until six this morning. It's a substantial list which may not prove to be helpful. In addition to officialdom and despite the yellow 'Do Not Cross' tapes surrounding the crime scene we've also attracted our share of voyeurs including my old friend Karl Malden who is working at a nearby sound stage on a film called 'The Phantom of the Rue Morgue'. I guarantee that nothing in his movie will be as gory as the corpse of Ivor Willoughby which is still hanging from the lamppost. I catch Malden's eye and he looks at me grimly, grabbing is throat and pantomiming nausea. Standing next to him is Merv Griffin, a former band singer with Freddie Martin, who has a small part in Malden's film. Griffin, too, looks a little green around the edges.

I turn as I hear a horn being honked and watch as a black Lincoln town car threads its way to the perimeter of the crime scene and stops. Byron Constable gets out from behind the wheel while Bob Fellows emerges from the passenger side. One of the car's back doors opens and Neville Waite steps out. I'd been wondering how long it would take for him to show up. The question is, why? Curiosity or to admire his handiwork?

Bob spots me and heads in my direction with Byron right on his heels.

"What happened, Joe?" he asks.

I tell him to the best of my ability. It's obvious that Fellows is also shaken. This kind of bizarre thing happens in cheap dime novels, not real life, and I can see that he is genuinely affected. I look at Byron. If he's shocked he does a good job of hiding it. Meanwhile Neville Waite has ducked beneath the yellow tape and is now a few feet from the body staring at it intently.

"Hey!"

Aaron has just spotted Waite and strides toward him in annoyance. I excuse myself quickly and try to cut him off but I'm too late.

"Sir, you don't belong here. This is a crime scene," Aaron says.

"I'm aware of that and I most certainly do belong here," Waite says dismissively.

I manage to step in front of Aaron before he gets a chance to throw the cuffs on Waite. After I introduce him, Aaron is still unimpressed.

"How do you do, Mr. Waite. Other side of the tape, please."

"Excuse me, Detective, but I am——"

"I know who you are and you have no official standing here so please move or I'll have you moved. And for future reference, it's Detective Sergeant."

"Very well, but I plan to report this incident to your superiors."

"I'm used to it," Aaron says.

"I've got him, Aaron," I say as I take Waite by the arm and guide him over to the side away from the center of activity.

"A friend of yours, Mr. Bernardi?" Waite sniffs.

"Very much so, Colonel. So what's it mean?"

"What?"

"The note pinned to the body. You seem like an Eton chap. Latin and Greek and all that other useless nonsense. What's it mean?"

"Literally, 'Thus to all traitors'," he says.

I nod.

"I guessed as much," I say. "And what do you think of the handiwork?" I continue glancing back at the corpse which just now is being cut down.

"Gruesome," he says.

"I suppose in your line of work you get used to things like that," I say.

"No, I don't," Waite says, "and I hope you are not intimating that savage torture is common practice for the SIS."

"I wouldn't know. I only know you came here to achieve justice for your government. Let me rephrase that. Dispense justice might be more accurate."

Waite glares at me.

"Surely you don't think me capable of something that sick

and depraved."

"I don't know you well enough to think anything, Colonel. although I have been told that you and a handful of others have certain powers granted to you by the Crown that obviate the need for arrest warrants."

"And who told you that?" he asks.

"A little birdie," I say.

"By the name of Finch?"

"Who?" I ask innocently.

"I know he's here."

"News to me," I say.

Waite sighs.

"Very well, Mr. Bernardi, I'll play your game. Let us say for the sake of argument that your feathered friend is right. "

"For the sake of argument, let's say that."

"What you see there is the work of a fiend, certainly not an officer in service to Her Majesty. If one of her agents were forced to act quickly and expediently on a quarry, he would most likely put a small caliber bullet into his or her brain directly behind the ear. Quick, painless and humane."

"In addition to sparing him or her the tiring agony of a trial by his or her peers."

"Why waste time and money when the outcome is not in doubt?"

"Oh, I don't know, . Maybe on the off-chance that Her Majesty's smug, self-serviing narcissistic bag of wind might somehow have made a mistake?"

Waite forces a cold smile.

"So nice to have met you, Mr. Bernardi. In case we don't meet again before I leave, I wish you the best."

He turns on his heel and walks off. I watch him go and and

as I do, I realize he's absolutely right. How could I be so stupid? MI6, like our own CIA, operates in the shadows doing everything possible to deflect attention from itself. No, this was something else altogether and that brings me back once again to the notion of extortion. Willoughby had some devastating evidence against someone and if he were smart he would have hidden the proof away someplace where it couldn't be found. Phoebe's bungalow was torn apart by someone looking for something and meanwhile Willoughby is in the hands of his victim who is determined to find and destroy this evidence. Willoughby is tortured mercilessly but does he talk or does his body give out before he breaks?

I look over at Nevlle Waite who is now standing with Bob Fellows and Byron Constable. They chat for a moment and then Byron takes out his pocket watch and checks the time and in that moment suddenly everything becomes clear to me. The three of them start toward the Lincoln town car and as they do, I hurry toward them.

""Byron!" I shout as he's just opening the driver side door. He looks toward me as I reach him.

"Look, I want to apologize," I say. "About my behavior yesterday."

"Unnecessary," he says.

I shake my head.

"No, I was way out of line and I'm very sorry. It won't happen again."

I put out my hand in a gesture of friendship. He hesitates and then takes it. His grip is firm and so is mine and then I reach over with my left hand and overlap the handshake like a Rotarian greeting a long lost buddy. Beneath his sweater and his shirt I can feel the bracelet and I don't need to be told what it looks like. It's made of copper and supposedly it wards off the pain of arthritis.

Our eyes meet and I know and as he looks back at me, his eyes cold as Pittsburgh steel, I know that he knows I know. We stand like that for what seems an eternity.

"Byron, come on. Let's go."

He turns his head. Fellows is exhorting him to get behind the wheel. I let go of his hand and he slips in behind the wheel of the car, giving me one last cold look before he starts the engine. I can read his expression. Starting now I'd best watch my back and considering what he did to Willoughby, it's a caution I take very seriously.

CHAPTER TWELVE

'm telling you, the son of a bitch killed him," I say.

It's past noon and the three of us are sitting at a table in the commissary having lunch. Me. Aaron. Pete Rodriguez.

"And you know this how, Joe? " Aaron says. "Because Constable doesn't wear a wrist watch?"

"That's part of it. Another part is the copper bracelet he wears on his right wrist."

"Which you didn't actually see."

"Didn't have to," I say. "I felt it."

"Oh, I see. You felt that it was copper. No chance that it might have been a silver plated ID bracelet or maybe a Navajo tribal bracelet or maybe some sort of Canadian good luck charm."

"I'm pretty sure it was a copper bracelet."

"Well, I have news, old pal," Aaron says. " 'Pretty sure' isn't going to cut it in a court of law any more than it'll rate inclusion in my police report." He takes a huge bite of his sloppy Reuben sandwich and spills cole slaw on his shirt. He mutters something ugly and wipes his front off with a paper napkin.

Rodriguez shakes his head.

"I know what you're getting at, Joe," he says, "but it really doesn't hang together. It's much more likely, given the note on the body, that Willoughby had defected to the Russians and this was somebody's idea of setting things right."

I shake my head.

"No, it's a diversion. Willoughby was blackmailing some-body he shouldn't have. Whatever documents he had, a diary or official document or photographs, they weren't enough to save him. Whether the blackmail victim has the evidence now we really don't know. Maybe Willoughby broke. Maybe he died first. Nothing else makes sense of the torture he endured."

"Again, you're guessing, Joe," Aaron says. "Evidence of what?"

"Willoughby tried to tell the military authorities about this flier named Smythe-Jones who he says betrayed an escape attempt from Colditz castle in which several of his friends were killed. Smythe-Jones was removed from the castle by the Germans the very next day. Years later when he tells his story the military tells him there was no Smythe-Jones flying for the RAF during the war. Okay, so the name's a phony. Now what about Constable? He was a Canadian attached to the RAF and flew bombers over Europe. He says he was shot down and spent the rest of the war in a prisoner of war facility. Colditz? Very likely. It was specifically set up to house British and American officers, principally aviators."

"Joe, again you're guessing," Aaron says.

"Constable used his influence to get Willoughby a part in the movie. What does that tell you?" I say.

I look from one to the other. I'm getting nowhere.

"Constable told Bob Fellows his Wellington had been shot down over Germany in November of '44. I know for a fact because I wrote a story about it for 'Stars and Stripes' that the Wellingtons stopped flying sorties over Europe in October of 1943."

"He misspoke," Aaron says.

"Misspoke, my ass," I say. "I think Smythe-Jones and Byron Constable are one and the same and he was either a flier turned traitor or he was a plant by the Germans who spoke perfect English."

Aaron and Pete remain unconvinced. They're cops. They think and act like cops and they don't deal in maybes and what ifs. I need something tangible to goose them into action. Until then, I'm on my own and it's a situation I don't much like. Constable is not about to forget about our handshake and worse, he may feel compelled to do something about it.

After lunch Aaron and Pete take off. I head for my office. I have phone calls to make and they won't wait. I'd just as soon Prunella Haworth and Phoebe Sweets not learn of Willoughby's death on the radio or television. Because the studio is private property, the reporters and news cameras couldn't get to the scene but it's only a matter of time before they sniff out the story.

I walk into my outer office and there he is, feet up on Glenda Mae's desk, drinking a cup of Glenda Mae's coffee. Alexander Finch throws me a smile of greeting.

"Morning, Guv," he says.

"How did you get in here?" I demand to know.

"Walked in," he says. "Thought I'd do a little nosing around early in the morning. Nothing better to do and I thought I might learn something. When I spotted the coppers all over the place I knew something was up so I skedaddled around back and walked through the delivery entrance. The gate was wide open and nobody there. So who's the bloke hanging from the lamp post? Did the Colonel get his man like I said he would?"

I jab a thumb in the direction of the door.

"Get out."

"C'mon, mate. All I want's a story. I hear you were once a newspaper reporter. How about a little slack?"

I walk to the desk and put my hand on the phone.

"You can walk out of here now on your own volition or I can call security who will take you into custody and then turn you over to the local police on a charge of trespassing."

When he doesn't respond, I lift the receiver.

"Smythe-Jones," he says.

I freeze.

"Who?"

"You know who," Finch says.

I lower the phone and then sit in the chair that adjoins Glenda Mae's desk.

"Okay, let's hear it," I say.

"It was in '47. I'd just started working for the Daily Telegraph and I'll tell you straight, I was a bit of a radical trying to make a name for myself so I write this story about all the cases where the SIS screwed up and let these Nazis and their sympathizers get away. Next thing you know three guys grab me off the street, take me to some basement and start beating the holy bejesus out of me. And here's this guy in a three piece suit smoking a cigarette and watching the whole thing like he was at some bloody fashion show checking out the quiffs. Yeah, that's right. Neville Waite. And finally when I'm down on the concrete spewing blood from my nose and my ears and God only knows where else, he leans down and tells me if I don't shut my fucking mouth, the next time he's going to kill me. And then he and his goons leave."

He stops to sip his coffee. His eyes are hard and cold now as he recalls the incident and what I see in his expression is raw hatred.

"He thought he had me scared," Finch says. "He was wrong.

He had me furious and from that day forward I made it my business to do what I could to bring Mr. High and Mighty Waite down from his perch. Whatever he did, whoever he interrogated, wherever he went, I had mates in the SIS who kept me tuned in. They despised him as much as I did but those poor blokes had to work with him. The interview with Ivor Willoughby? That was Waite's work though he probably wouldn't admit it. Secrecy is their mother's milk. They wouldn't admit their eyes were brown if you were staring them in the face."

"So Waite knew about Smythe-James," I say.

"He knew what Willoughby had said about him but I doubt he believed him. Waite was trying tio make a case that Willoughby had been turned against the Empire by the Soviets. Smythe-James didn't fit his agenda so he dismissed him."

"But you didn't."

"I did not," Finch says. "In those days if Waite said hot, I said cold. If he turned left, I turned right. I was contrary to the core trying to catch him in a huge mistake."

"And so you went looking for Smythe-James."

Finch nods.

"Or at the very least other Colditz prisoners who could back up Willoughby's story. I managed to find a half dozen of them and to a man, they supported Willoughby."

"Did you catch up with Smythe-James?"

"No, but I got a pretty good description," Finch says. "Six feet tall, blonde hair, blue eyes, almost Nordic looking, and a small red crescent shaped birthmark on his cheek."

I try not to give myself away but he has just described Byron Constable. I stare at Finch and wonder if I can believe him and of course I know I can.

"Well?" Finch says hopefully.

"Do you have affadavits?"

"I'm not stupid, mate. They're back in London."

"Do you have someone who could fax them to me?"

"I might."

"And I might tell you what's going on if you agree to feed the story to your London paper and nowhere else, especially not here in L. A. ."

"That might work," he smiles.

I spend the next thirty minutes telling him everything I know and even what I surmise. He takes copious notes writing furiously in shorthand. When I'm through he uses my phone to call a friend named Sheila Noone in London and gives her explicit instructions on where to find the affidavits. He supplies her the Warner's fax number and tells her to direct the material to my attention.

When he's finished I get up and walk him to the door and shake his hand. I tell him I hope this works out well for us both. He assures me it will. He has Neville Waite in his sights and sooner or later, next month or next year, he promises to bring Waite down. God may have created man and woman and heaven and earth but in Finch's opinion, if He created MI6, He should be ashamed of Himself.

I return to Glenda Mae's desk. I don't have Prunella's home phone so I call her office number and tell her answering service to contact her immediately and call me back as soon as she's able. Urgent. I leave both my numbers as well as Jillian's. I have better luck with Phoebe. She's home. As gently as I can I tell her what has happened.

"I knew," she says. "If he'd still been alive he would have called me, he was that kind of person."

"I'm really sorry, Phoebe. I know how much you cared for him."

"Yes. Well, life goes on, Mr. Bernardi. Wylie will always have a special place in my heart no matter what."

"Good for you," I say. I have spared her the gruesome details. She doesn't need to hear them.

"Mr. Bernardi," she says. "One thing. You said if I thought of anything or came across anything that might be strange, I should let you know."

"Absolutely," I say. "What is it?"

"The key."

"What key?"

"The one on my key ring. I just noticed it this morning. It's a little brass key and it's not mine and I don't know where it came from."

"Are you sure?"

"Positive. What should I do?"

I glance at my watch. It's well past two o'clock now and I'm running out of time. I'm supposed to be at Jill's by three o'clock. I'd like to take a close look at this mystery key but I have no time.

" I can't get away right now so suppose you just hang onto it and I'll call you tomorrow."

"I can do that," Phoebe says.

"Good girl," I say. "Till tomorrow then." And I hang up.

The Saturday traffic is not good. Thirteen days until Christmas and the shoppers are out in force. I'm bumper to bumper going over Sepulveda, most of the time stuck behind a car that has a huge Douglas fir strapped to its roof. I'd have better luck trying to see past a tractor-trailer. And even as I fight the urge to lean on my horn, my radio is playing 'Have Yourself a Merry Little Christmas. ' I punch in a new station and get assaulted by Rudolph. Is there nowhere I can hide?

I pull up to Jill's at precisely five minutes to three. A cab is parked at curbside and the driver is leaning against the hood reading the afternoon paper.

"Been here long?" I say to him as I head for the steps.

"Half hour," he says, barely looking up.

"You got the meter running?"

Now he looks at me.

"Is the Pope Italian?"

I nod and hurry up the steps. Before I can even pound on the door it opens and Jill is standing there, a look of mild annoyance on her face.

"You're late," she says.

I show her my watch.

"Two minutes to three. I'm on time."

"You know perfectly well when I say three o'clock that I don't really mean three o'clock," she says.

Did I mention that Jill is anal about time and appointments? If she's going to a 7:00 showing for a picture that got panned by every critic in the country, she will arrive at the theater at 6:30 to make sure she gets a good seat.

"Sorry," I say. "It won't happen again."

"You're forgiven," she says with a smile, giving me a little hug and a peck in the cheek. We go inside.

Yvette is in her playpen, rattle in hand, beating the stuffing out of Pooh Bear. When she sees me she giggles. She is very proud of herself. I tell Jill that these aggressive genes are none of my doing. She gives me a dirty look and leads me upstairs.

The house has changed a lot since I first met Jill. The upstairs guest room closest to Jill's master suite has been converted into a nursery complete with bassinet, bathinet, crib, dresser with eight drawers, a changing table, a box for toys, wall shelves for dolls, hanging mobiles and an auxiliary portable playpen. Anything that

Man has invented for the safety and comfort of a new born baby is in this room somewhere. There are two battery operated baby monitors, one at each end of the room, and just to be on the safe side, Jill has had an open archway cut out of the wall between this room and her own bedroom. I am told by Jill to sleep in her bed this evening. The sheets are fresh as are the towels in her bathroom.

For my convenience she has laid out several play outfits as well as a dozen diapers. The baby powder and baby oil are sitting on the changing table along with a dozen safety pins. This is so I won't have to run around the house looking for something. We go back downstairs. In the kitchen she has lined up a half dozen jars of baby food and a box of pablum. Yvette's bottles are on another counter along with several cans of formula. Across the room is a bulletin board on which she has tacked a phone number for the pediatrician and a map showing how to get to the local hospital. Having carefully oriented me, she now feels safe in leaving. I get another quick hug, a sisterly peck on the cheek and out she goes, promising to be back no later than noon tomorrow. I watch as she climbs into the back of the cab and throws me a last wave goodbye and then the cab is heading down the street. I close the door. Now at last, a chance to get really acquainted with my daughter without her meddling mother hanging about.

When I enter the living room, I see that Yvette has tired of her assault on Pooh Bear. In fact she's just plain tired. She's scrunched up in a ball, thumb in her mouth and fast asleep. I watch her for several minutes, so peaceful and innocent and my heart aches a little because I know that moments like these cannot last. After a while I sit down quietly in a nearby easy chair. I glance over at a book Jill has left for me to read. Dr. Spock's Baby and Child Care. She doesn't miss a trick.

CHAPTER THIRTEEN

True to her word, Jillian returns at noon and I am delighted to see her. It's not that I didn't enjoy my day with Yvette because I did but I learned several valuable lessons I won't soon forget. First of all, caring for a nine month old baby is no easy chore even with help from a nanny like Bridget. The little dear is demanding and doesn't take no for an answer. When hungry she cries. When wet or poopy, she cries. When full of gas she cries until she is properly burped. Even when hungry she sometimes displays the bad manners of a finicky eater. What? You don't like peas? When did that start? How about some nice squash? Okay, I'll open another one. How about this pretty red jar? Beets. Yummy. Aha, I've found something she likes. And then there's her other end which needs tending to at the most unexpected times. I have also discovered that sleep can be a luxury. Last night I got about six hours. Two, two and two interrupted by crying in one case (wet diaper) and odd noises coming through the baby monitors in the other two which spurred me to leap from my bed to investigate in an abundance of caution.

When you get to right down to it, there's not much you can do with a nine month old except rock it in your arms, softly coo lullabies. talk baby talk to it and then watch it behave like a baby, a pastime that gets old really fast. I guess my idea of fatherhood to a daughter has a lot more to do with watching her learn to walk and talk and then dress up like a little lady and learn to ride a bike and take dance lessons and go off to the junior prom with some guy you wouldn't otherwise trust to take your garbage to the curb.

"How was she?" Jill asks.

"An angel," I say.

"No problems?"

"None."

She smiles.

"Thanks, Joe," she says. "You're a life saver."

"Untrue. Lydia would have volunteered in a second. Matter of fact, she probably did so I thank you, Jill. This was really generous of you."

She comes to me and we embrace and hold onto each other for quite a while before she breaks away.

"I think she is very lucky to have such a caring and thoughtful Uncle Joe. She's going to grow up loving you as much as I did and still do." We stand like that for a moment and then she says, "I guess you'd better go."

"I guess I'd better."

I pick up Yvette and give her a hug and then hand her to Jill.

"Anytime, Jill," I say.

"You bet," she says. "How's your Christmas?"

"Just another Friday."

"Dinner's at three. How do you feel about Virginia Ham?"

My heart jumps a little.

"Is that an invitation?" I ask.

"How dense are you, Joe?"

"I'll be here," I grin.

"Thirty dollars tops on any present," Jill says.

"As always," I say.

"As always," she says giving me a knowing look.

I'm home before one and pull into the driveway looking forward to an hour's worth of nap time. I park the car in the driveway and head for the side door that opens onto the kitchen when I see it. A business card is tacked to the door frame and when I look closely I see the door has been forced open with a chisel or a crowbar. The card belongs to Pete Rodriguez. On it he has scribbled 'Call me'.

"Joe!"

I turn and my next door neighbor, Chuck Bledsoe, is striding towards me.

"Are you okay?" he asks.

"Fine. What happened?"

"You had unwelcome company last night. I was getting ready to hit the sack when I looked out my window and saw this guy—I guess it was a guy— at your side door and the next thing I know he's in your house waving a flashlight around. I figure it's not you so I call the cops. About five minutes later a squad car pulls up out front and I guess the guy must have spotted it because he comes tearing out the kitchen door and across Santini's back yard and he's gone."

I open the door and Chuck and I go inside. At first glance nothing's been trashed and as far as I can see nothing's out of place. I call Pete and he tells me he'll be on the scene in ten minutes. I offer Chuck a cup of coffee which I could use myself. I put it in on the stove and while it's percolating Chuck and I start looking through the house which looks relatively undisturbed.

When Pete arrives we cover the same ground. No, there's nothing missing as far as I can tell. When he makes the mistake of asking me if I have any idea who the intruder was, I start in again on Byron Constable.

"That's a guess," he says.

"Yes, and a damned good one," I say.

Pete turns to Chuck.

"Any way you could identify this guy if I showed you a picture?"

"Not a chance," Chuck says. "Much too dark."

He looks back at me.

"We could dust for prints but I have a feellng that's a dead end."

"Me, too, but you might want to ask Constable where he was last night around midnight."

Pete smiles.

"I could do that, Joe, but I have this nagging feeling he might lie to me."

"You think? So what are you going to do?" I ask.

"There's not much I can do," Pete says, "except to have the local patrol car pay special attention to this place on their rounds."

"Don't bother," I say.

I'm annoyed but I know Pete's hands are tied. He has nothing to go on and realistically, he has no cause to go after Constable except for my unfounded claim. After he and Chuck leave, I take one more look around and discover nothing new. I check the drawer of my nightstand. My .25 caliber Beretta automatic is still there. I take it out and slip it into my pocket. For the time being, where I go, it goes.

I return to the kitchen where I take a long look at my wounded door. I'm not a carpenter and even if I were I have neither the time nor the tools to repair it. I grab the knob and push it as tightly shut as I can. I just manage to slide the dead bolt in place. As a means of entry and exit it's now worthless. The first chance I get I'll have one of the studio carpenters come by and take a look at it. This is one of the little known perks of working as an executive for a movie studio.

I'm just finishing my second cup of coffee when the phone rings. I lift the receiver.

"Hello?"

"Mr. Bernardi?"

I recognize her voice.

"Phoebe?"

"I've been waiting for your call," she says.

Damn. I'd forgotten all about her.

"I still have the key but I have to be at work in a half hour. What do you want to do?"

What I want to do is take a nap but I'm too wired now to think about rest. Constable has declared war and I am not about to play defense when what I really need is a good offense.

"Suppose I meet you at the station," I say.

"Sure. That'll work. Do you know how to get here?"

"I do," I say. "I'll see you in about an hour."

It's nearing three thirty as I tool down Sunset Boulevard. A perfect sunshiny day is turning into something else and I kick myself for not checking the weather report. I turn into the Paramount Sunset Studios where KTLA maintains its operations. Because it's Sunday, the parking lot is nearly deserted and I park close to the main entrance. Inside I ask at the desk for Phoebe who is expecting me. The security guard gives me directions and I wend my way through a couple of corridors toward the studios at the rear.

Stage 6, I am told, is the stage that was used to film the original 'Jazz Singer' twenty-six years ago when Warners owned the facility. Now it belongs to Paramount as does KTLA. Phoebe is sitting in a director's chair with a clipboard on her lap and a stopwatch in her hand and she's taking notes. Her face still shows traces of the beating she'd endured but makeup has masked most if it.

There's something being filmed this afternoon. It looks like a syndicated show called 'Dixie Showboat' though I wouldn't swear to it. Anyway the whole operation looks very much like a Warner's movie set only more chaotic.

I put my hand on Phoebe's shoulder and she looks up at me with a smile.

"Hi," she says.

"Hi, yourself," I say. "Busy?"

"I can take a couple of minutes." she says. "Let's get some coffee."

She gets up and we walk over to the far end of the stage where craft services has set up a table. We grab coffees and find a couple of chairs.

"I really don't know if this means anything or not," she says, as she fumbles around in her purse, "but you said anything unusual and this is unusual. At first I thought it was strange but meaningless and then I realized that for whatever reason, Wylie had put this key onto my key ring without telling me. I asked myself why. I have no idea."

She removes a brass key from her key chain and hands it to me. It is plain with no identifying text or number. It's not a safe deposit box key because I know what they look like but it could be just about anything else. I turn it over in my hand, puzzled.

"What do you think?" she asks.

"I don't know," I say. "He said nothing about it, not a hint?"

"Nothing."

I think about Willoughby's recently rented apartment where Pete Rodriguez and I searched what little there was to search and found nothing. I think about Phoebe's little bungalow being tossed as if a runaway train has plowed through it. And then I think of Poe's "The Purloined Letter" where the vital letter in question couldn't be found because it was right out in plain sight. Clever fellow, that Willoughby. Hiding a key on someone else's key chain.

"I'd like to hang onto this," I say to Phoebe.

"Sure," she says.

"Whatever I come up with I'll let you know," I say.

She nods. Then quietly, she asks, "Did he suffer much, Joe?"

I hesitate.

"I don't know Phoebe. I think maybe his heart gave out very quickly. I hope so."

"So do I," she says sadly. Something catches her eye and I see a man waving to her. "I have to get back to work."

"I'll call you," I say and walk away.

Out in the parking lot I slip behind the wheel of my car but I don't start the engine, Again, I turn the key over in my hand. An extra key to the recently acquired apartment? Possibly. A storage unit somewhere? Maybe, but what would be so large that he'd need a storage unit? It's not a car key and it's too large for one of those small fireproof boxes for valuable papers and even if it weren't, where's the box? Finally I decide I can't really get anywhere until I eliminate the new apartment so I fire up the engine and head for the corner of Highland and Santa Monica.

There are a couple of tots playing on the sidewalk when I pull up to the curb in front of the apartment house. They're deep into an invigorating game of potsy and I do my best to avoid stepping on their grid. I look up into the sky and I think maybe the kids' game is about to come to a premature halt. The clouds are turning black, heavy with water, and a shower can't be far off. I hurry up the inside staircase and walk to the end of the corridor. I hear a few Sunday sounds of people enjoying a day off from work, arguing about the dinner menu, and watching or listening to Sunday sports. No sound comes from 2G as I slip the key into the lock.

I try to turn it. It won't turn.

"Hey!"

A loud voice reverberates through the empty hallway. I turn and see Novak, the building super, approaching. Today a white shirt and a suit are covering his undershirt. He's even wearing a tie. As he gets close I see that he still has his cigar between his teeth and it's still unlit. I see also that he recognizes me.

"You were here the other day. With the police," he says.

"That's right, Mr. Novak. With the police," I say misleadingly. "How long has your tenant here got to go on his lease?" I ask.

"Lease? What lease? He paid two weeks in advance. If he don't show by Friday, he's outta here."

"He won't be showing," I say. "Pack up his stuff, stick it in the basement for now and rent the place out."

"He skip town?" Novak asks.

"Dead."

If this comes as a big surprise, he doesn't show it. He just nods. "That'll do it."

"I don't suppose he might have given you something to hold for him, for safe keeping?" I say. "Like a strongbox, something like that?"

"You gotta be kidding," he snorts.

"Forget I mentioned it," I say.

As I exit the apartment building the storm clouds have really

137

started to gather. It is turning dark and the wind is whipping up. I hop in my car and slide in behind the wheel. Okay. Not the apartment. Now what?

I look across the street as a little VW pulls up to the curb and a funny little man in a sweat shirt and sweat pants and a baseball cap gets out and hurries into the post office. This seems strange because it is Sunday and the "rain and sleet and dead of night" motto doesn't really apply on weekends. It gets even stranger when the guy reappears a couple of minutes later with a handful of mail which is when I realize he has checked his post office box. The counter may be closed but the box section is always available seven days a week any time of the day or night. I still have the brass key held tight in my fist. I open my hand and look at it. Now I'm beginnng to think Willoughby was a genius. Too bad he wasn't smart enough to keep himself from getting killed.

I get out of my car and jog across the street just as the first raindrops begin to fall.

CHAPTER FOURTEEN

s soon as I enter the post office box area, I am dismayed. A quick estimate tells me there are more than six hundred boxes. With no identification on the key, I face a gargantuan task. But then it occurs to me that it could be worse. All of the boxes have glass windows for easy inspection and I have no interest in an empty box. Ditto one that is stuffed with mail. If I am right the box I am looking for will hold one and only one letter.

I start at the top left hand corner of this bank of boxes, skipping the empties and trying the key in all the others. Thirty minutes later my patience is rewarded. The door opens and I reach in, extracting the one letter within. It is addressed to Wylie Wyckham, P. O. Box 191, West Hollywood. There is no return address.

I move down to the far end of the small room where the light is better and tear open the envelope. It is a lenghty letter written in a sort of cramped longhand but it is legible. I begin to read.

To whom it may concern: If you are reading this, then I suspect that I am dead and my best laid plans have come to naught. Too bad. I knew when I embarked on this course I was taking a risk but it didn't bother me. I've been taking risks all my life. I probably should have been shot down a dozen times during the war but somehow came through. Maybe I've been on borrowed time ever since. Never mind. This letter is not about me, it's about a man who once called himself Henry Smythe-James and lately has been going by the name of Byron Constable. Both names are false. While this man was going by the name Smythe-James he was responsible for the death of eight good men, all of them my friends. An escape from Colditz castle had been planned for January 1945 and Smythe-James knew all the details. The men never made it further than a hundred meters from the castle when they were set upon by the guards and their dogs. The next morning the Gestapo arrived. Two days later a rump trial was held for the eight leaders who were found guilty and lined up against a wall and shot to death. By that time, Smythe-James had already been removed from the general population. We were told he had been transfered to another stalag.

Four months later American forces arrived at Colditz and we were liberated. Euphoria reigned but not for long. Colditz is located in what became known as the Russian sector and the G. I.'s were forced to leave and the Russkies took over. We'd hoped for speedy repatriation. We didn't get it. In some ways they were a lot like the Nazis only less polite. Fed up, me and two of my buds decided to make a break for it and in July we got out and I made my way to Dijon, France, to reunite with a lovely French woman who had aided me in my darkest hour. I probably should have made an effort to go home to England but truth be told, there was nothing there for me. Mom and Dad were killed in the early bombing and my fiance didn't survive a strafing of Topcliffe airfield in Yorkshire. So I stayed with Blanche.

It was in the summer of 1948 that I ran into Otto. Otto had been a guard at Colditz during its final year. He'd been old then, replacing a younger man who found himself shipped to the

Russian front, and now Otto was even older. He'd always been soft spoken and genial and because he spoke English we got to know him. Like us, he wanted it over with so he could go back to his grandchildren in Hamburg.

With the war only a memory, we sat down and talked about the days at Colditz and that was when I asked him what had happened to Smythe-James. He raised his eyes heavenward and then, at my urging, told me all about the man we thought was one of our own. It turns out he was something of a legend among the German POW camps.

His real name, Otto said, was Andre Trevallier from the little town of Sainte-Adele north of Montreal. Father French, mother German. They had emigrated to Canada after WWI and bought a small farm where Andre was raised with his two younger sisters. He learned to speak flawless French and German in a household where hatred for the British ran deep, at least as far as Andre's mother was concerned. The war came along and Andre, who had no great love for farm labor, enlisted in the Canadian Air Force and after several months training was shipped off to England to replace RAF pilots who were being shot out of the sky like clay pigeons at a skeet shoot. He survived the Battle for Britain but his luck ran out in late 1942 when his bomber was riddled and he was forced to chute down over France. He was picked up immediately and turned over to the Gestapo for questioning. Andre had heard the stories of brutal torture and he didn't need much persuasion to cooperate. In any case, his mother's anti-British indoctrination had already kicked in and he eagerly volunteered his services to the Reich.

Otto said to me, you can guess the rest. They shipped Andre around from prison camp to prison camp where he passed himself off as a recently downed flier while all the time feeding information to the camp commandant. His final stop, apparently, was Colditz. We shared a final schnapps and then Otto took his leave and I never saw him again. Meanwhile, my well ordered life took a body blow. Blanche's husband, whom she thought had been killed in a partisan raid on an ammunition dump. showed up, minus one leg but otherwise in good shape and it was time for me to go. At that point I resolved to get back to England because I had something vital to report and I was excited that my eight friends who died against a prison wall would finally be avenged.

But the new boys in charge of the SIS were no longer interested in what happened in a Nazi prison camp over three years ago. No, it was all about the Russians and espionage and especially about 'the bomb'. So after two days of answering their questions and getting nowhere in my plea that they open an investigation on Smythe-Jones, I walked away and found my way to Manchester.

It was there that I met Wylie Wyckham, a pleasant outgoing young man who was operating a barely profitable theater group. He knew I was on my uppers so he invited me to move in with him. For a split second I worried that he might be a poof but not so. I did the cleaning, shopping and washing to earn my keep and after a few weeks he asked if I'd like to have a go at some stage work. So I did and I found out I not only liked it but I was pretty good at it. Jump forward a couple of years. The SIS still had me on the books as a possible Communist conspirator and though they hadn't come close to finding me, there was always that chance they'd stumble across me by accident. And that's when Wylie had an accident of his own, drowning while on holiday with his fiance in Scotland. I mourned with everyone else but I also saw my chance to get out from under. With Wylie's *passport and other documents and a little alteration here and there, I used his identification to make my way to America to begin a new life. I knew only two skills: shooting down Jerries and acting and since Jerries were out of season I tried to make it as an actor. It has been damned hard.*

Then came Remembrance Day. You Yanks call it Veteran's Day. I'm in the lobby of a movie theater waiting to buy a soda when the man in front of me turns around and I find myself face to face with Henry Smythe-James. I'm startled and so is he because I can tell immediately he recognizes me. I stifle an inclination to cry out for the police and greet him civilly and because I do, his guard is down. After the film we get together for drinks and I can tell from his clothes and his demeanor that he's in the chips. When he mentions that he is the right hand man to a powerful motion picture producer, a thought crosses my mind. I tell him I'm an actor and could use a decent part. I can tell he's going to shine me on so before he gets a chance to say no, I tell him about my encounter with SIS in '48 except I frame it like they are looking for Smythe-James and I have played dumb. Buddies stick together, don't they? He gets the hint and says he'll arrange for a part in this picture they'll be starting in a week.

Several days later I know the name he is using—Byron Constable—and we meet for dinner at some tony tourist trap that's always crowded. My idea because when I tell him what I have in mind, he won't be able to come across the table at me with the nearest sharp instrument. I mention his birthplace, his German mother, his collaboration with the Nazis, his betrayal of his countrymen in various POW camps. I can see him pale at each revelation. He knows I have the goods. I ask for only five thousand dollars. Just enough to move into livable digs and get myself a decent wardrobe for making the rounds. I won't need

more. I won't ask again. And oh, yes, I tell him I have it all writ-
ten down and it is being held in a safe place. Whether he believes
me or not, he comes up with the five thousand.

Two weeks later, the picture rolls. I am photographed in sev-
eral scenes at the Glendale Grand Central Air Terminal whch is
doubling for San Francisco. I arrange for another dinner. He tries
to beg off but I warn him not to. This time I ask for fifteen thou-
sand. I need a new car and a membership in Hillcrest Country
Club. This was two days ago. I am awaiting his response. It is
my intention to bleed him dry of every dime he owns and then
report him to the SIS. This letter is my insurance against the
possibility of retaliation. To be honest I have no idea what he is
going to do. What will be will be.

This is all of it as I know it. Most of this information can
be easily verified through Canadian, British and German war
records. Whoever reads this, remember. Eight men are looking
for justice. I may be the ninth.

Respectfully,
Lt. Ivor Willoughby
602 Squadron
Royal Air Force.

Slowly I refold the several sheets of the letter and replace
them in the envelope, then slide the envelope into my inside
jacket pocket. The poor bastard. He played a dangerous game
and he lost but I can't fault his bravery. Maybe he'd have been
better off just going to the SIS immediately but I think the idea
of making Constable squirm was too good to resist. Well, his
squirming days are almost over. Now comes the weeks and
months of fear as the hangman's noose hovers over his head. I
couldn't be more delighted. This barbaric son of a bitch is finally

going to get what's coming to him.

I go through the door and step out into the darkness. The rain has abated slightly but I wish I had an umbrella. Next stop, Aaron Kleinschmidt.

"Bernardi!"

I turn at the sound of my name. Constable is standing in the shadows. He moves into the light and I can see the revolver he holds in his hand, unobtrusive, close to his leg. A silencer is attached to the barrel.

"I'm parked down the street," he says. nodding his head to his left.

"Good for you." My right hand moves instinctively to my pocket and then I remember that when I got to KTLA I put the Beretta in my glove compartment to avoid any problem with their security people.

"We can make this hard or easy." He moves toward me until we are less than a foot apart. There are people around but because of the rain they are few in number and scurrying to get to a dry place.

"You're not going to shoot me. Not here."

"Don't be so sure. Without that letter I have nothing to lose." He waits. I don't move. "Don't doubt me, Bernardi. One shot to your chest and you fall like a stone. I rush to your side and retrieve the envelope from your jacket, all the while calling out for help. A crowd gathers. I say you've had a heart attack. More people crowd in. As they do I rise and back away and then slip away down the street to my car. Maybe you'll survive. Maybe you won't but I don't care because I have the letter. Now decide."

I am looking at my car across the street but I can't chance it. Everything I know about this man says he will pull the trigger in a heartbeat. I move away from him and start to walk slowly down the sidewalk. He stays several paces behind me. I see his Cadillac dead ahead. I wonder if I have made the right choice. I wonder if I have any choice at all.

CHAPTER FIFTEEN

onstable has ordered me behind the wheel while he sits in the passenger seat holding the gun. The rain is light but it's steady and the roads are shiny with moisture. On Constable's orders I head west on Santa Monica until I reach Coldwater Canyon Avenue, then head north over the hills and down into the Valley. I head east and then turn into Balboa and start north. I have no idea where I am going. I know only that my captor has a pistol in his lap and it's pointed directly at my midsection.

"I don't want to kill you, Joe. Not unless I have to," Constable says, finally breaking the silence.

"Nice to hear," I say. "Christmas spirit?"

"Self preservation. I'm sure you've already made an issue of me with your police friends. Should you wind up missing or dead, I would come under a lot of scrutiny which I would just as soon avoid."

"Can't say I blame you."

"Willoughby was a zealot. There was no dealing with him. I have a feeling you might be more persuadable."

"Could be."

I'm going to humor this guy from now to New Years if that's

what it takes while I try to figure a way out of this mess. We cross Devonshire still heading north. Dead ahead is the sleepy little town of Granada Hills. Orange groves. Farms. Small ranches. Patches of forests and fields. I think they have one traffic light. Maybe two. Overpopulation is not one of Granada Hills' problems.

We cross Rinaldi Street. It's very dark now and very wet and there are tall evergreens on both sides of the road. Civilization is in my rear view mirror.

"Up ahead on the left, a billboard for Esso. Turn left just before it," Constable tells me.

I do as he says. The road is dirt and rutted and the Cadillac jounces badly. My headlights cut into the inky blackness caused by the overhanging trees. I slow to a crawl. I pass a few small ramshackle houses which are set back off the road. Half are dark. The rest have one or two lights visible. A nice area for a gathering of hermits. Suddenly the road takes a sharp turn and then another and then to my right I see a clearing and a small one story house. Actually it looks more like a cabin.

"Turn in here," Constable says. "Pull up close to the door."

I obey and cut the engine.

"Home sweet home?" I ask.

"For the time being," he says. "Out."

I step out of the car into the mud that makes up the clearing. Constable exits from the passenger side. He waves the gun in the direction of the front door of the little house.

"You first," he says.

I do as I'm told and reach the door.

"I don't have a key," I say.

"You don't need one. As soon as you open the door, reach to the right for the light switch and flip it on. Then slowly take three steps forward and stand very still."

Again I do as I'm told. When the low wattage wall lights go on, I'm startled by what I see. This is the main room of the house and it is basically unfurnished. For a table, he has set up two empty nail barrels and stretched an old beat up door across them. Two straight backed chairs are positioned next to this makeshift table. Nearby is an ancient stuffed easy chair now with less stuffing than the day it was manufactured. Against the wall is a small wooden table atop which sits a small screen television set, no bigger than 10", with built in rabbit ears. To the right of the front door is an alcove featuring an ancient refrigerator and a built in shelf on which sits a dual hot plate unit. I've heard of no frills. This is absurd.

Constable has followed me into the room and closed the door.

"I sense you're unimpressed. I'm satisfied with it. The rent is cheap, the landlord minds his own business and doesn't ask for documents and I have no curious neighbors to fend off. When my position within the industry becomes more secure, I will make adjustments. Until then, this is, as you put it, home sweet home."

"I know rats who live better than this," I say, turning to face him.

"I'm sure. Now place the letter I saw you reading through the post office window on the table and then go over against that wall and sit down."

"How long have you been following me?"

"Ever since you arrived at your house today from wherever you spent the night."

"My address isn't public knowledge."

"No, but as one of the producers of a motion picture being filmed on your lot, it wasn't hard to come by. The envelope. On the table, please."

"I assume that was you who visited me last night."

"You assume correctly and count your blessings you weren't at home. I'm pretty sure that last night you had no idea where the letter was and therefore it would have gotten messy and painful finding that out. For you, not me."

He looks past my left shoulder and points. I turn. The door to one of the bedrooms is open. My stomach tightens as I look upon the bed, it's sheets all mussed up and soaked with blood. Ropes attached the four corner posts of the bed now lay loose and there is a large open tool box on the floor at the bed's foot. I look back at Constable.

"Did you have to kill him?" I ask coldly.

"It wasn't deliberate. I think his heart gave out on him. No matter. If he'd told me where to find the letter I would have had to kill him anyway. He brought this on himself, you know. I don't know which annoyed me more, his self righteous need for justice or the blackmail. And Joe, if I have to ask you one more time to put the letter on the table, I will shoot you and take it from your dead body."

That sounded an awful lot like a threat so I did as I was told and then walked over to the far wall and sat down, facing him.

"Back tight up against he wall, please, and legs crossed."

I hesitate, then comply.

"Excellent. From that position, you will not be able to successfully make a move at me before I can put a bullet in your brain. You also save me the chore of tying you up which I would rather not do."

"Thanks."

"No need. It's physically impossible to bind you without knocking you senseless first and again, that is a barbaric way to proceed, especially if you and I are to reach an accommodation. As I said earlier, Joe, I would rather not kill you if I don't have to."

He switches the pistol to his left hand and unscrews the silencer which he places on the table. He lays pistol next to it and shrugs off his jacket, never taking his eyes from me. He's right. I have no chance of jumping him. Whatever he has in mind, I'll just have to play along. Now he slips out of his vest, being very careful with his silver pocket watch and then he sits down and picks up the envelope. He removes the pages and starts to read, one eye on me and the other on the letter. I sit very still.

I look around the room and try to assess my chances of escape. They are not good. I estimate him to be twenty five feet away. A frontal attack with his pistol so close at hand would be suicidal. The bloody bedroom is closer. Maybe twelve to fifteen feet. And next to the bed is a window that looks out over the rear of the property. No, it's still too far. Directly across from me and next to the open door is a closed door which I am pretty sure opens onto a bathroom. Maybe if I could make a move toward the bathroom—

My thoughts are interrupted.

"Yes, that's pretty much how it was," Constable says, laying the letter on the table. "Now let's talk about your future, Joe, and I sincerely hope you have one."

"Talk to me," I say.

"First of all you're much too young and much too bright to still be working for Jack Warner."

"He pays me well," I say.

"But for how long? You should be branching out, getting into film production, as an executive or a writer or a director. You have many options and I can make it happen."

"Can you? Are you speaking for both Wayne and Fellows?"

"Wayne is no longer relevant and Fellows does as I suggest. I know that Bob thinks the world of you."

"Nice to hear, but the Duke irrelevant? Hard to believe," I say.

"He's planning to buy out Bob and start a company of his own called Batjac Productions, I believe. Bob will be heading up his own firm with me at his side and you on board, if you are so inclined."

"And what's the deal?"

"Fifty thousand dollars as a signing bonus, a vice presidency in the new company with a salary to match, and five percent of the stock."

"And of course, I forget all about that letter and anything else I may know in connection with Ivor Willoughby."

"Naturally," Constable says.

Suddenly the room is saturated with light as a huge sheet of lightning hits right outside the little cabin. A moment later a blast of thunder rocks the walls. The rain has morphed into a full fledged storm and we are located in the heart of it.

"You're hesitating, Joe. Surely this decision cannot be that hard. I am offering you life and success and money and power. The alternative is unthinkable."

"No, no. It's just that thunderstorms make me nervous."

"There's not a lot to think about. I seriously doubt you had a deep rooted relationship with Willoughby. Surely you can't be toying with some misbegotten notion of loyalty. To a black-mailer? Come, come, Joe, you cannot be considering jeopardizing your life and the lives of your loved ones for a principle."

Again lightning, just as close, followed immediately by a crash of thunder overhead.

"Loved ones? What loved ones?" I ask warily.

"I saw the picture in your bedroom last night, Joe. The framed photo of the very attractive woman with the child in her arms." Jill and Yvette taken a month ago.

Fear seizes me but I stifle it immediately and force myself to laugh.

"You're nuts," I say.

"Am I?"

"I bought that frame at Woolworth's last week. The picture came with the frame. I have no idea who those people are."

Constable's eyes turn to piggy little slits.

"And whose picture do you plan to put in that frame, Joe?"

Again, I try to think quickly and logically. Constable is quick and he's no fool and I'm having trouble thinking clearly. My legs, which had been hurting from my cramped sitting position, now are starting to numb up. Even if I get a chance to run for it, will I be able to?

"My mother. She's mailing me her photo from Oklahoma."

Constable shakes his head sadly.

"Joe. Joe," he says. "You never had a mother. Anyone who's read your book knows that. Nice try, though. So who's the woman in the frame?" I don't answer because I don't know what to say. "Seriously, Joe, how long do you think it would take me to find out who she is. Less than a day, I can promise you, I'm very good at that sort of thing."

"She has nothing to do with our arrangement," I say.

"Not true," Constable says. "You see, if we strike a deal you might feel compelled at some future date to turn on me. But I don't think you would do that if I made a solemn vow that I would kill both woman and child in an instant as punishment for betrayal. Am I right about that, Joe?"

I say nothing. The last time the lightning struck, the lights on the wall flickered slightly. A solid hit and maybe the power will cut out. Unobtrusively I start kneading my crossed legs, trying to restore circulation, hoping for an opportunity.

"Please, Joe. Don't fight me on this," Constable says. "You're not a fool. You know you have no choice."

Again the lightning strikes outside the cabin and this time the lights flicker and go out. As the thunder cracks in the gloom above us, the room is thrown into blackness. I throw myself forward, uncrossing my legs in the process and try to scramble to my feet. My legs have barely any feeling in them but I force myself forward and scrabble toward the bedroom door. For just a moment or two Constable has no idea where I am and I pray that the next lightning hit will hold off for just a few more seconds.

Still scrabbling along the floor I am almost to the bedroom door when the lights come back on. I turn in panic and look back at Constable who has the pistol in his hand and is grinning at me. He raises the pistol.

"This was your choice, Joe. I'm very sorry," he says.

And then as quickly as they had come back in, the lights once again go dark and in that split second I lurch forward even as I hear the ear splitting report of Constable's pistol and a bullet whine past me, only inches from my head. I'm on my feet and stumbling toward the bedroom window, old and weathered and paned. I duck my head down and cover it with both arms as I dive toward it, head first. Wood splinters and glass shatters as I tuck and roll when I hit the muddy clearing. I skid forward on the slick surface and slam into a tree stump. I feel a sharp pain in my rib cage and I know I have done damage. I roll over and look back at the house as Constable appears in the bedroom window. He sees me and raises the pistol. I scramble to my right.

Ten yards of clearing and then the forest resumes. I slip and slide, flailing for traction. Two shots ring out. I feel a tug at my jacket sleeve and then a sharp pain in my arm. Another bullet whines harmlessly overhead and then I am into the trees and fighting my way through the underbrush, away from the cabin and towards God knows what.

CHAPTER SIXTEEN

I can barely see where I am going. These woods are dark and I grope my way, half walking and half crawling, through sopping wet underbrush and low hanging branches that slap me in the face as I go by. Every thirty or forty seconds lightning strikes again and for a moment I can see what's ahead. I lurch toward open spaces. I desperately pray I find some sort of dirt trail so I can make some headway. I know Constable is on my tail because when I look back I can see a flashlight bobbing to and fro, searching everywhere. My arm is throbbing and my ribs send constant stabs of pain throughout my body but I know I cannot stop because to stop is to die. And yet how much further can I go? Already the pain is reaching into my brain and I am feeling disoriented. I have no idea what is beyond the next bush or the one after that but I know I must keep moving.

More lightning. I freeze in place for a moment until darkness returns and then I continue on, staying low, affording Constable no target if I can avoid it. The rain is cold as it beats down heavily and every part of my body and clothing is soaked. I start to shiver and look back. The flashlight is closer now. Constable is on his feet and unhurt and, inexorably, he is closing the gap. In a matter of minutes he'll be in top of me. I continue scrabbling forward. My hand falls in something long and hard. I try to examine it. It looks like a two-foot length of copper pipe. I grip it tightly and then make for a nearby bush. I scrunch down out of sight and wait. Byron Constable and his pistol are heading toward me. I will have one chance. If I fail I will be dead. I have to risk it. If I don't I'm dead anyway.

I listen intently as I peer through the branches of the bush, my eyes fixed on the flashlight. The light is all I see. Only the light and then it stops moving and slowly scans the area. I hold my breath. I will myself to total immobility.

Suddenly, lightning. The forest lights up like an arcade for a brief moment. Constable whips his head around peering in every direction within a matter of a second or two. He, too, is drenched, hair soaked and matted, shirt clinging to his body like a bad paint job. His right hand clenches the pistol, his left the flashlight. He starts to move. For a moment he seems to be walking away from me but then he stops and comes back. The noise of the rain and whistling of the wind drown out most sounds. Only his eyes will be able to locate me as he moves forward. He draws closer and closer to where I am hiding. He stops a foot away. If he looks down to his right he will see me. I can't wait.

I take dead aim at his knee and lash out with the pipe.

Even through the noise of the rain spattering on the trees and on the soaked ground cover I hear the crack and feel his leg give as he screams in pain and falls backwards into the mud. I rise up and lurch toward him, then freeze as I see he is still holding the pistol. He looks up at me, wild-eyed. a combination of pain and rage. He raises the pistol but it's now covered in mud and it slips badly as he squeezes the trigger and the bullet plows into the ground. I back away, tossing aside the pipe, and then start to hobble back into the underbrush.

"I'll kill you, you son of a bitch!" he screams.

I don't look back. Move forward, I tell myself. Watch where you're going. Look for a road or a house, anywhere that might be safe. The rain is coming down harder now and another sheet of lightning illuminates the forest. I ignore it. I slip and fall to my knees, then get up and keep moving. I continue on, then allow myself a quick look back for any sign of the flashlight. It's a mistake. Suddenly I find myself in mid-air, free-falling and then rolling and tumbling down a hillside, down, down, falling over rocks and debris until I come to a sudden stop, splashing in water. Lightning strikes again and I realize I have hurtled down a steep embankment and ended up in a swollen stream of foot deep rushing water. I try to get up but I can't. My right leg is useless. I have either broken something or it's sprained. Either way I am immobile. I look up toward the top of the embankment and I see a wavering light approaching slowly. Constable has been slowed but he hasn't been disabled. He is coming toward me, still carrying his damned pistol.

If the lightning holds off until he passes I might be okay but if it hits and he looks down, I'm an easy target. I tense as he approaches the ridge. Just then I think I hear voices. Maybe it's the wind playing tricks. Then another shout and a shot rings out. I look up and see Constable, flashlight in hand, and then he collapses out of sight. A man rushes forward from out of the darkness. Another man follows him. They are both wearing uniforms. They bend down, disappearing from view, tending to the fallen Constable. I raise my head and shout but they don't hear me. One of them stands. I scream as loud as I can just as lightning strikes once again. The man in the uniform must have heard me because he looks down. Thunder rumbles overhead and then the beam of a flashlight stabs through the darkness in my direction. I manage to raise my arm and wave. The last thing I remember before I pass out is a uniformed cop scrambling down the embankment in my direction.

It's no longer dark. My eyes flutter open and look up at an expanse of white. It takes me a few moments to realize it is a ceiling and I am in a bed in a hospital room. I examine myself as best I can. An IV is dripping into my left arm. My right arm is bandaged just above the elbow. It throbs a little but I'm in no pain. My right foot and ankle are heavily bandaged and in traction. When I lean forward for a closer look I feel a sharp pain in my torso and I am aware that my rib cage has been tightly bound. I lean back and smile. I'm alive and if I'm lucky that son of a bitch Constable is dead. I close my eyes concentrating on one of my last memories. Voices. A shot rings out. Constable slumps to the ground. I smell jasmine. That's odd. I don't remember smelling jasmine.

I open my eyes and a beautiful face is inches away from mine, peering at me intently. It breaks into a smile.

"Awake. I thought so," she says. "How are you feeling?"

"Not awfully good, not awfully bad. Where am I?"

"St. Joseph's Hospital," she says, whipping a thermometer from out of nowhere just like Mandrake the Magician and jamming it into my mouth. "Under the tongue," she says.

"Owong ibn ayr?" I ask.

She must hear this a lot because she answers immediately.

"Two days. And be quiet or you get no breakfast."

I shut up for the next two minutes while she inspects my arm bandage. When she finally takes out the thermometer, I ask, "Will I live?"

She makes a production of examining the temperature reading and then shrugs noncommittally.

"Touch and go," she says. And then she again gives me that beautiful smile. I check out her name tag.

"Thanks, Hannah, I'd like a second opinion."

"Okay," she says, "it's fifty-fifty."

"Better," I say. "I'm Joe."

"I know," Hannah says. "So does most of Los Angeles." She wraps my left bicep in a blood pressure sleeve and starts pumping.

"What are you talking about?"

She reaches into the night stand next to the bed, takes out a newspaper, and hands it to me. It's the L. A. Times dated Tuesday the 15th which apparently was yesterday. The headline reads: TORTURE KILLER ARRESTED and beneath that a smaller subhead: "Warner Brothers Executive Rescued from Watery Grave." The by-line belongs to Lou Cioffi, the paper's ace crime reporter, who writes the way he talks in clipped prose and bellicose phrasing.

"He's not dead," I say.

"Who?"

"The man who tried to kill me."

She shakes her head.

"No, he took a bullet in the shoulder. We kept him overnight. Right now he's in county jail. What do you want for breakfast?" she says, unwrapping the blood pressure sleeve.

"Two eggs over easy, four strips of bacon, a buttered danish, orange juice and black coffee."

"We have chicken broth or beef consomme, red jello or green jello, dry toast and hot tea."

"I'll take it," I say irritably.

"Which?" she says.

"All of it," I say, "and make it double everything. I'm starving."

"You're also a masochist," she says, heading for the door. "Read all about yourself while I see if I can find your doctor."

I smile, watching her leave the room. She boasts a cute little wiggle under that starched uniform and she knows it. When she's gone I turn my attention to the paper.

To say that Lou got it wrong is an understatement but I'm sure a lot of people were lying to him. It's also obvious he was doing a lot of guessing. In Lou's narrative I was a kidnap victim for reasons which are not clear. My captor was a studio executive whose name is being withheld pending further investigation. No mention is made of extortion or blackmail nor does Lou cover Willoughby's letter of self-protection. I doubt he knows about it, There are enough entities involved like FBI, LAPD, SIS and CIA to make a good sized bowl of alphabet soup and until these competing factions get the facts sorted out, secrecy is everything. Still you have to hand it to Lou. His ability to create a front page story out of thin air is mind boggling.

My doctor makes his appearance while I am polishing off my second cup of red jello. His name is Blandings and he's a bug-eyed little man who reminds me a lot of Peter Lorre. His favorite expression is "We'll see" which he uses in response to all of my questions such as 'How long do I have to stay here?' and 'When can I go home?' and 'What are the chances of getting a sirloin steak for supper?'

He tells me I am a very lucky man. The gunshot wound to my arm is superficial but I lost a lot of blood before I could get to the hospital for treatment. My two cracked ribs will bother me for a while but they should heal nicely. My right ankle is severely sprained. I will be on crutches for at least a week. I again ask when I can exit the premises and I won't take 'We'll see' for an answer. He breaks down and says possibly tomorrow if I have someone at home to take care of me. I ask if Hannah is available. He stares at me blankly. Blandings lives in a world of gunshot wounds and broken bones and is oblivious to everything else.

My first real visitor walks through the door at 10:30. Jill is carrying an arrangement of carnations and yellow roses. She stops short when she sees me.

"My God, you look like crap," she says.

"Ah, but living crap," I say.

"Have you looked in a mirror lately?"

"No," I say. "They're also keeping me away from sharp objects. How bad is it?"

"Dark circles under your eyes, bruises on your chin, a three day growth of beard and your hair looks like a bird's nest."

"Any stitches?"

"None I can see."

"What a relief."

Jill takes the flowers and arranges them in my water pitcher. They look great. I just hope I don't get thirsty.

"Where's the baby?"

"Home. You didn't think I'd bring her here, did you? This place is full of sick people."

"So I guess Bridget's back from the wedding. How'd it go?"

"The wedding was fine. The reception afterwards was a disaster. Bushmill's and Guiness flowed like water. Two guests ended up in the hospital and five went to jail including the groom who took a swing at the local postman who made a pass at Bridget's mother."

"And her a blushing bride. Wish I'd been there," I say.

Jill nods.

"You would have fit right in. The doctor says you're fit to leave tomorrow."

"Wonderful. I can stop formulating escape plans."

"I'll pick you up at ten o'clock."

"Thanks, Jill, but I'll grab a cab."

"No, you won't," she says, "You're coming home with me."

I shake my head.

"Oh, no, I couldn't," I say.

"You can and you will or you stay here. Doctor's orders."

"No, that would really be imposing."

"Shut up and be grateful," Jill says. "Between me and Bridget, we'll have you covered."

She comes close, leans in and kisses my cheek.

"Ten a. m. Don't keep me waiting."

She turns and out she goes. My protest was all show. A few days with Jill and the baby. It could be a lot worse.

Within a few minutes, the phone calls start coming through. The Duke's among the first. He congratulates me on my toughness and invites me out for a sail on his fishing boat with Jack Ford as soon as I'm ambulatory. He tells me he always knew that Constable was a slimy piece of work though he admits he doesn't really know what's going on. I promise to fill him in as soon as I'm free to do so. Ray Giordano calls. So do Lydia, my ex, and her husband Mick, one of my guy-pals. Glenda Mae shows up with a big bag of chocolate chip cookies secreted in her oversized purse. She describes herself as a semi-professional hospital visitor who knows how the game is played. She is glad to see me alive and well but also tells me that I look like crap. All my girls have a way with words.

Lou Cioffi also calls and while he is polite I can tell he is unhappy. He knows that his story in yesterday's paper is cotton candy and his professional pride is wounded. He wants the real scoop and tries to wangle a face-to-face if I'm up to it. I tell him

I am but my hands are tied. There's too much I can't talk about because of the ongoing investigation. Maybe next week, I say. Maybe next week we can use the story for wrapping fishes, he says, as he hangs up angrily. I feel bad. He's always played ball, even when it was ethically risky for him. I hope he doesn't stay mad long.

At ten to noon, Aaron finally puts in an appearance. I'm relieved to see him. Now I may actually find out what's happening.

In answer to my question, he tells me that Byron Constable is, indeed, in county jail.

"We're holding him on a charge of kidnapping and attempted murder for the time being while we sort out the other charges."

"You saw the inside of his cottage," I say.

"Godawful," he says. "Forensics went over it for hours. The blood in the bed matched Willoughby's type."

"And you got the letter."

He nods, pulling up a chair.

"Found it on the makeshift table. It's legitimate. Willoughby's prints were on it as well as Constables."

"Not your run of the mill homicide, is it?" I say.

"Hell, no," Aaron growls. "I've got the FBI and the CIA all over me, not to mention that arrogant prick from London. I expect a phone call from Eisenhower any day now telling me to play nice with the jerk."

"So tell me how you and your boys saved my life. You had me followed, right?"

"Wrong," Aaron says. "You were so damned adamant about Constable I authorized a tail on him for seventy-two hours."

"You DID pay attention," I grin.

"Stop patting yourself on the back or you'll break your arm,"

Aaron says. "My guys saw you get into his car outside the post office. Why you did that I do not know."

"He had a gun on me," I say.

"Oh," Aaron says. "They missed that. Anyway they followed the Cadillac north, past Granada Hills but in the dark, they missed your turn off. They knew you were around somewhere so they stayed close and when one of Constable's neighbors reported gunfire, they were back in the hunt. By the time they got to the cabin, you were already being chased through the woods. When they heard another shot, they went after you."

I nod.

"And got there just in time," I say.

"Apparently so."

"Thank 'em for me."

"I will."

"So, how hush-hush is this business, Aaron?" I ask.

He shrugs helplessly.

"Ed Lowery is trying to convince me it's an FBI case which it isn't. The slug from the CIA who has no business being involved is getting in everybody's way and this Neville Waite guy is running around screaming extradition when he hasn't a single scrap of paper to back him up. Days like this I wish I were back in the traffic division."

"Non carborundum illegitimus," I say.

"What's that? Latin?"

I nod.

"Loosely translated it means, 'Don't let the bastards wear you down.'"

He laughs.

"I won't," he says.

And I know he won't. It'll take more than the British

government and America's security bureaucracy to intimidate Aaron Kleinschmidt.

He gets to his feet.

"I hear you're getting out of here tomorrow."

"You hear right."

"I need you down at division for a statement."

"No problem."

"Then I'm going to put Constable in a lineup. Until we build the murder case we've got him only for kidnapping you so we need your official identification. It's a formality but we need the paperwork."

"I'l be there," I say. "Anything to salt this guy away for the rest of his life."

Aaron gives me a little wave and heads for the door. When he's completely out of sight I reach under the covers and take out my bag of cookies. When it comes to chocolate chips, I share with nobody.

CHAPTER SEVENTEEN

t's just past ten in the morning and Jill is helping me get dressed. Except for the brief moments I get to flirt with Hannah, I can't wait to get out of this place. My room has turned into a hothouse for every variety of flower known to man. Half are from good friends. The other half are from actors and actresses who want to stay on my good side. Making and keeping valuable contacts is an art form in this business. Most performers are good at it. I give Hannah my permission to send the flowers around to patients who are alone in the world or ignored by so-called loved ones.

The barrage of phone calls and parade of visitors continued yesterday afternoon and ended long after I had half eaten my inedible supper. Jack Warner called and spared me seven minutes of his time. I was a genuine hero. He was proud of me. And finally, he warned me, don't do it again. He's tired of telling me not to play cop, especially on company time. He loves me like a son and he doesn't want to lose me and by the way, does that knucklehead who works for me have any idea what he's doing? I assured him that Dexter is very capable and when he wanted to know when I was going to be back at my desk, I told him in a day or two. That seemed to satisfy him and he hung up without saying goodbye. Working for Jack Warner is never predictable and is certainly never dull.

Bertha Bowles also called, full of concern for my well being and wishing me a speedy recovery. She did not once mention her idea of collaborating with me in a new venture and so I assume that the idea of a partnership was a passing fancy and nothing more. I also heard from Dexter who seemed overwhelmed at having to assume my duties as well as his own. I know what he's going through. He's afraid of making a mistake so he puts things off. I tell him it's the wrong approach. Think it out. Decide. Do it. Most of the time you'll get it right. That seemed to make him feel better but the other half of his problem is Jack Warner and that I can't help him with. He sounded relieved when I told him I'd be back soon.

Lydia and Mick put in an appearance along with Ray and Trudy. Cassie Ryan from casting brought me a pint of Cutty Sark, just in case. Harry Davis dropped by. He didn't have much to say except how good I looked. He told me that four times and then he left. I gave him the Cutty Sark. Don't much care for scotch. Visiting hours run to 9:00 and I was ready to tuck in for the night when Alex Finch popped through the door. He had doughnuts which was reason enough for me to greet him warmly. I was still hungry after that lousy dinner I'd barely dabbed at. I bade Alex pull up a chair while I bit into a chocolate glaze with sprinkles.

Finch was fascinated by the little he'd heard of my adventure at the hands of Byron Constable, aka Henry Smythe-James nee Andre Trevallier. He wanted all the details for his readers back in London. When I hesitated he reminded me that he had supplied me with a lot of valuable information I otherwise wouldn't have had. I had to agree and so on the continuing condition that the story appear only in the London Daily Mail, I told him about my ordeal.

He was fascinated, especially when I revealed the contents of Willoughby's lengthy letter. He took notes furiously in shorthand on a little pad. I told him about the bloody bedroom. He seemed sickened. He could only shake his head when I described running through the woods with Constable right behind me, firing at me, intent on murder. When I finished he stared for a long time at the notes on his pad. Unbelievable, he kept muttering. Finally he looked up at me and asked if I was convinced. Did I believe that Constable was this Smythe-James who worked hand-in-hand with the Germans to betray the Allied prisoners of war? Would I risk a libel suit from Constable to tell my story? I said there was no doubt in my mind. Nor in mine, he had said as he slowly closed the notepad. He smiled at me with those stained crooked teeth and told me I had done the world a great service. His readers will be told in great detail the sort of patriot I have become to the British people. For a fleeting moment the thought of knighthood flickered through my brain. It disappeared just as quickly.

And now Hannah is in the room with the wheel chair. I need this to get to the front entrance. Without it I will be trapped here, perhaps for the rest of my life, because hospital regulations are bent for no man. I climb aboard wearing the fresh clean clothes Jill has brought me. My other clothes are in a bag which I hold in my lap along with my new crutches. Jill is carrying what is left of my bag of chocolate chip cookies. I warn her I have done a count. No poaching allowed.

As we approach the front door, I suddenly have a vision of Jill's tiny yellow VW beetle but I needn't have worried. As soon as we are clear of the door a handsome older gentleman in a dark suit has taken my clothes bag and crutches from me and we are heading toward a shiny new stretch limousine parked at curbside. Leave it to Jill to think of everything. I wish Hannah a sad farewell and she responds by slipping me her telephone number. If Jill is put out by this, she doesn't show it. Meanwhile, Freddie, he of the dark suit, helps me into the rear of the limo. There is enough room in here for a cricket match, even after Jill slides in next to me. In a moment or two we are on our way to Parker Center and a rendezvous with Aaron Kleinschmidt.

Aaron's in an office on the third floor and I get there with a minimum of inconvenience. Crutches and I are old friends. I've had two broken legs so I'm an excellent hobbler. Jill is waiting downstairs in the lobby. Freddie is standing watch over the limo. Aaron rustles up a cup of hot coffee for me and then we get down to business. A steno takes it all down and thirty minutes later Aaron has his statement. He'll have it typed up while I'm at the lineup and then I can sign it before I leave.

As I start to get up, a familiar figure appears in the open doorway to the office. Neville Waite favors me with an icy smile.

"I'd heard you were in the building, Mr. Bernardi," he says. "Congratulations."

"For what?"

"Staying alive," he says.

Aaron's on his feet.

"You'll have to excuse us, Mr. Waite, we're kind of busy right now."

"I won't take up any of your time, Sergeant. I'm just here to fill out some papers before I fly home. I have a five o'clock flight to Heathrow aboard BOAC"

"Sorry you didn't get your man, Mr. Waite," I say.

"But he was gotten for me, Mr. Bernardi, and the Crown was

spared the nuisance of a trial. All around, a good result."

"I disagree. Ivor Willoughby was no more a Soviet agent than I am. The real disgrace to your British Empire is sitting in a cell in county jail."

"And I would like to see Mr. Constable get what's coming to him, but I am not authorized to remain here any longer. I commend him to American justice and hope for the best. Gentlemen."

With a curt nod to the two of us, he leaves.

Aaron shakes his head.

"Every time I meet a Brit like him, I am so grateful that we beat the crap out of Cornwallis at Yorktown."

"I second that opinion," I say as we leave the room.

We take the elevator down to a lower floor and Aaron escorts me into a small room where we find a man who introduces himself as Constable's lawyer. I look for horns or a forked tail and see none but I'm pretty sure he has them well hidden. One wall of the room is dominated by a curtained window and when the curtain is drawn back I find myself looking through a one-way mirror at a raised platform which is used for standard police lineups. Five men enter from the left and take up positions side by side by side. Constable is in the middle. I refrain from screaming out "Number Three! That's the son of a bitch!" I'm pissed but I respect the protocol.

Not so Constable. The officer in charge is giving instructions to each man in order. Step forward. Turn left. Turn right. When he gets to number three, Constable lunges forward, screaming at the window.

"Is that you in there, Bernardi? You bastard! You stupid fuck! I should have killed you back at the post office. I'm gonna get you if it's the last thing I do!"

Almost immediately, two uniforms have hopped up on the

platform to subdue him. Not only that but the other four men in the lineup join in the fracas. I find out later they are all police officers in civvies. He's still screamng when they haul him away. I look over at Constable's lawyer who is trying to melt into the woodwork. I turn to Aaron and deadpan it. "Number Three," I say quietly. "I'm sure of it."

Having signed my statement I head for the lobby. When the elevator doors open, I spot Jill. She's sitting on a bench chatting with Lou Cioffi. Do I really want to deal with Lou right now? Do I really have a choice?

Jill gets up to greet me. So does Lou who throws me a smile which reeks of insincerity.

"All set?" she asks.

"All set," I say.

"Don't suppose you've got a few minutes, eh, Joe?" Lou asks.

"I really don't, Lou," I say.

"Well, find them," he says sharply.

I hesitate, then turn to Jill.

"Could I meet you outside?" I say.

"Sure," she says. "But don't be long. You need rest,"

I tell her five minutes, no more, and off she goes. I look back at Lou.

"Lou, I—"

"I'm trying to think back to the number of times I let you and Dick Tracy manipulate me into using my column to help you catch bad guys. Do you remember, Joe? How many was it? Three? Maybe four?"

"Okay, okay. I'm an ungrateful weasel."

"Make amends."

"I can't."

"Nice phrase. I'll remember it next time you need something," he says as he starts to walk away.

"Lou! Wait!" I call and hobble after him.

"I can't talk to you," I say. "You're local. There's a police investigation going on. Talking to Finch was an entirely different matter."

His ears shoot straight up like a bird dog on the scent.

"Finch? Who's Finch?"

"A reporter for the London Daily Mail," I say. "He fed me a lot of information. I felt obligated to fill him in with everything I knew."

"Everything?"

"Absolutely but I wasn't really interfering with the investigation. His report was going straight into the London paper and nowhere else."

Lou nods slowly. He's starting to get it.

"London Daily Mail, you say," Lou says.

"Right."

"Monday edition?" he asks.

"Probably. Maybe Tuesday," I say.

"I might use it for research,"Lou says.

I take this to mean he'll soon be deep into blatant plagiarism. He knows it and I know it and he knows I know it.

"You're such a tickler for ethics, Bernardi. It's a wonder I deal with you at all." he growls.

"My Boy Scout upbringing," I say.

"Lucky for me I stumbled upon that news story in the London paper," he says.

"Sometimes God is good," I say thoughtfully.

"He certainly is. Well, I'll see you around."

"Take care."

And off he goes with a jaunty walk.

I limp out the front entrance. Jill's already in the limo and Freddie is standing by the rear door. He opens it for me and I slide in. Jill gives me a dirty look.

"Are you through?"

"With what?"

"You get yourself released from the hospital so that you can rest and convalesce. You go to police headquarters where you spend an hour giving a statement, then participate in a lineup and a few minutes ago you start chattering with the press. Now are you through?"

Chastened, I say I am through and we head for home. Halfway there I fall asleep. Maybe Jill's right. Maybe I've been overdoing it just a little.

CHAPTER EIGHTEEN

Climbing the stairs to the second floor of Jill's house was a bit of a chore but once I made it to the top, my worries were over. The guest bedroom on the far side of the nursery has been refitted with a hospital bed and all the amenities. There's a rolling tray that I can pull up over my lap to eat from or prop a book on. Alongside the bed is a night stand with a strong lamp for reading and a pitcher of ice water. Jill's even put an extra phone line in so I can do business over the next couple of days. A nurse call button is looped around the bed frame and is set up to buzz next to Jill's bed if I need help in the middle of the night. At the foot of the bed on a table is a decent sized television set. The only drawback is, I need someone to come in and change channels for me should I want to go from one station to another. Maybe in the future some electronic genius will come up with a device that will make that unnecessary.

Bridget Mary Margaret O'Shaugnessy has been hovering over me like a mother hen since the moment I walked in the door. She's not Hannah but she'll do. At 63 she is grey-haired, outgoing and optimistic, a walking encyclopedia of Irish folklore and superstitions. She has an herbal cure for everything except the 'Irish disease' for which she says there is no cure, short of closing down every pub in the country. If there were her people wouldn't be over there murdering each other in the name of Christ Almighty. She used to come mornings and leave by four. With the birth of the baby she has become a live-in. Jill added a large bedroom and private bath to the rear of the house and now she is a member of the family, indispensable in every way.

While I am in the bathroom changing into pajamas and a robe, Bridget is turning down my covers and fluffing my pillows and making sure that the bed is canted at just the right angle. Yesterday Jill had gone by my house and packed enough things for a week's stay as well as Ernie Gann's "Soldier of Fortune" which I have not yet finished reading. She tells me my car is in the garage having been picked up by the police and driven there from the post office where it had been parked.

I slide into bed and get comfortable. I assure Bridget that I'm fine and need nothing. Not coffee, not tea, and not hot soup. I pick up my book and turn to a dog-eared page. Reluctantly Bridget exits the room and with a sigh I start to read. It's a good story, full of excellent characters and for at least ten minutes I'm mesmerized but not so mesmerized that I don't fall asleep with the open book in my lap. My mind may be willing but my body is shot.

I'm awakened shortly past six by Bridget who has brought me a plate of fried chicken, mashed potatoes, peas and a tall glass of orange juice. I try trading in the juice for a Coors but she'll have none of it. Jill comes by a half hour later with a dish of vanilla ice cream and carrying Yvette under her arm. We let the baby crawl around the bed for a few minutes while we chat about the twists of fate that have brought me to this point. Jill suggests that I might endure a lot less trauma in my life if I stopped minding other people's business. I concede the point but there's something inside of me (some in our business would call it a character flaw) that won't permit me to let an injustice go unchallenged. There are too many Byron Constables in the world, too few Ivor Willoughbys. That sort of equation has to be dealt with.

By eight-thirty I've had enough. Jill tucks me in and douses my overhead light. I give Gann another go, knowing I'll probably doze off again and it almost happens. I hear the phone ring in Jill's room. It doesn't ring in mine because Jill has disabled the ringer to make sure my sleep isn't disturbed. After a few moments Jill appears in my doorway.

"For you," she says. "Some man who wouldn't give his name but he says it's important."

I nod. Probably Lou Cioffi or Alexander Finch. I pick up. "Hello."

For a moment there is silence and then he says, "I promised I would kill you and I will."

Every muscle in my body tightens.

"Do you hear me, Bernardi? I'm going to kill you. You and that woman and that child. All of you and I'm going to enjoy every minute of it."

"How did you get this number?" I manage to say very quietly.

"It wasn't hard," Constable says. "When I checked your personnel file for your home address the other day, I noted this number for emergencies. Where are you, Joe? I came looking for you but you're not here."

"What do you mean, not here? Where are you?"

"In your kitchen, of course. Using your phone. I'm disappointed, Joe. I was hoping to find you in."

"Consider yourself lucky you didn't," I say with a bravado I don't really feel.

Constable laughs.

"Really, Joe? I admire your gall but against me you'd stand no chance."

"Try me."

"Oh, I will, Joe. First chance I get. And when you see the lady and the kid, say hi to them from me."

He hangs up.

"Jill!" I scream it at the top of my lungs. In a moment she's back in my doorway.

"What is it? What's the matter? Why are you yelling?" she asks.

"Are the doors locked?"

"Yes. Always."

"What about the alarm system?"

"Not until I'm ready for bed," she says.

"Set it now," I say.

"Joe, I—"

"That was Constable, Jill. He's out of jail. He just threatened me."

"My God," she says, turning pale. She hurries away from the door and down the staircase. I reach for the phone and dial a number I know by heart.

"Hello," Aaron says after two rings.

"Aaron, what the hell is going on?" I ask.

"Joe? Jesus, where are you? I've been trying to locate you for the past two hours."

"I just got a call from Constable. He's in my house, Aaron. He's threatened me and Jill and the baby!"

"Dammit," Aaron growls. "At four o'clock this afternoon some brain dead Judge granted Constable bail. At six o'clock his lawyer showed up with fifty thousand in cash and Constable walked out the front door. Where the hell are you?"

Aaron knows all about my situation but I never told him Jill's name. Now I have no choice. I also tell him the address.

"I'll have a patrol car there in ten minutes and I'll be there inside of an hour. Sit tight. Don't do anything dumb."

"Hadn't planned to," I say as I hang up.

I slide out of bed and slip into my bathrobe and grab my crutches. I make my way out the door and ease my way slowly and carefully down to the bottom of the stairs. Jill hurries toward me. She looks terrified. She knows all about what Constable did to Ivor Willoughby.

"It's okay, Jill," I tell her. "He doesn't know this address, only the phone number. There'll be a police car outside in a matter of minutes and Sergeant Kleinschmidt's on his way."

"The baby—!"

I drop my crutches and take her in my arms, holding her close.

"The baby will be fine. We're in no danger. He was calling from my house. That's thirty minutes away even if he knew this address which he doesn't."

I can feel her shaking and I know it's not fear for herself but for Yvette. Bridget appears from the kitchen area where she's been cleaning up. I tell her briefly what's happening without details. She's unfazed by the potential danger but she dials in on Jill's panic.

"I'll go upstairs and see to the little one," Bridget says as she brushes by us and strides up the staircase. Her tone is matter of fact but there's no doubt in my mind she'd throw her body between the baby and danger if it ever came to that.

Seven minutes later an LAPD squad car pulls up to the curb

and two uniformed officers hurry up the steps to the front door. Jill lets them in and I quickly fill them in on the situation. They grasp it immediately and the junior of the two goes outside to scout the grounds while the senior officer takes notes for his report. It's shortly before ten when Aaron arrives. I introduce him to Jill whom he's never met. By now she's more herself knowing that a professional police presence is on the scene. While Bridget continues to watch over Yvette, Jill puts on coffee and we sit down in the kitchen to discuss options. The uniforms are camped in the living room.

I say I could go to the judge, tell him about Constable's threats and maybe get his bail revoked. Aaron thinks that unlikely. It'll be my word against his and that won't be enough to put him back in a cell. It's possible the department might authorize a 24 hour surveillance on Constable but something like that is merely short term. Jill doesn't want to move and uproot the baby, even temporarily. She can afford round the clock security on the premises and is ready to go that way if need be. There is, however, one thing I know and that is the fact that I can no longer stay here and put both Jill and Yvette in danger. How I am going to handle that I do not know.

Aaron leaves shortly before midnight promising to return at eight in the morning. He's arranged to have our two cops relieved at four o'clock. This presents no problem. None of us is thinking about sleep, certainly not me. I alternate between reading and working crossword puzzles in an L. A. Times anthology. The rest of the time I stare at the ceiling, wondering how I got myself into this mess and how I'm going to get myself out of it.

The clock edges toward three a. m. and I look over at Jill who is dozing, sitting up, on the sofa. This is one great lady and I know it so why can't I be in love with her the way I am with the long missing, wayward Bunny Lesher. It's been nearly four years since I've seen Bunny. In that time I have talked to her on the phone three times for a total of seventeen minutes. Wherever she is and whatever she has become I know that I am still a part of her and because of this I cannot let go. I wish I could. I wish I could say, to hell with you, Bunny Lesher, go your own way and stay out of my life. Set me free to learn to love Jillian Marx and to marry her and raise our baby in a proper family setting. That's what I wish for and I know there isn't a prayer in hell of it ever coming to pass.

At 6:30 Bridget starts to rustle up some breakfast for all of us including our two new cops. Jill is on the phone to Mick Clausen whom she awakened from a sound sleep. Mick is married to my ex-wife Lydia and runs his own bail bond company near City Hall. This makes him familiar with every low life aspect of living in L. A. and when it comes to a private security company he can recommend one without reservation. Jill asks for the number but Mick goes her one better and says he will call on her behalf and give the owner, an old friend, Jill's phone number. Expect to hear from him right away, Mick says.

Sure enough, by the time Aaron arrives at five to eight, Jill is on the phone with Mick's pal, Zeb Faubus. Whatever Faubus is saying must be hitting all the right notes because Jill has thrown off her fears and when I catch her eye, she smiles at me and gives me the old thumbs up.

Aaron and I make our way into the kitchen and over bacon and eggs, we discuss my options. He agrees with me on one thing. I can't stay here another minute more.

"I can always place you in protective custody," he says,"but I doubt you'd like the accommodations."

"Amen to that," I say.

"A good hotel is always a safe bet if you're careful but it's expensive and if Constable's patient he can wait you out."

I nod. Short of charging him with first degree murder and the possibility of the death penalty, it's doubtful his bail will be revoked. And if his lawyer's any good he can delay and delay so that months may go by before he'll have to stand trial. No matter how nice the Biltmore is, I'm not ready for week after week of living in a hotel room. I realize that time is on Constable's side. We're playing a game of cat and mouse and the mouse doesn't set the rules. Somehow I have to change that.

I sop up the last of my egg yolk with my remaining piece of toast and sip some hot coffee. I see one way to bring this to a head and only one.

"I'm going home," I say to Aaron.

He hesitates for a few moments and then nods.

"Okay. We can handle that," he says.

"Thanks, good buddy, but there's no 'we' involved."

He looks at me sharply.

"What are you talking about?"

"I mean, I'm going home and you have to stay out of it."

"Are you crazy? Do you want to get yourself killed?"

"Not if I can help it. Look, Aaron, if this guy is as loony as we think he is, I have to draw him out right away and better I take him on at my place than here or somewhere out in public. I'm in no condition to fight or to run but I can defend my home if that's where he comes for me."

He shakes his head.

"I can't let you do it."

"You have nothing to say about it," I tell him. "We have to get this over with now. If he thinks I'm an easy target he'll come after me and one way or another we'll be done with it."

"What makes you think you can handle this guy?" Aaron asks.

"What makes you think I can't? I qualified 'Marksman' with a. 45 automatic while I was in the service."

"That was ten years ago. Besides Constable's not a paper target."

"You're wasting your breath."

Aaron glares at me. He's furious.

"You stupid bastard, do you think this is some kind of a game? People who play with guns die, You make a movie with John Wayne and suddenly you become a damned cowboy. My God, Joe, wake up."

I just shake my head slowly, .

"Unless I stop him, unless I kill him, he'll come after Jill and the baby. I have to do this, Aaron, and I will do this."

Aaron falls silent. Finally he says, "Let me put a man in the house with you."

"No."

"He'll stay out of sight. Constable will never know he's there."

"He'll know. He's not stupid. No man in the house. No unmarked car a block away waiting to rescue me. No squad cars patrolling the neighborhood. Nothing, Aaron. My fight. Let me fight it."

"I can't let you do this alone."

"You want to help? I'll give you something to do. Send one of your techies over there and wire the place. Put a van ten blocks away in the shopping center. You listen in. If something happens, make sure you record it. One way or another we'll get this guy."

Aaron glares at me again.

"You mean if he kills you we'll have him dead bang for murder one."

"That's the deal. Take it or leave it."

He hesitates for a long time.

"Get dressed," he says finally. "Pack your things while I talk to my techie."

It's nearly one o'clock. I'm dressed and sitting on the sofa. My travel bag is sitting by the front door along with my crutches, Aaron sits by the phone waiting to hear from his techie. Jill has been told that I am going to spend a couple of nights at Aaron's place just to be safe. Everyone's on board with this including Zeb Faubus who looks at my continued presence here as an impediment to good security. Faubus has come up with a terrific plan. Outdoor sensors have been strategically placed. Anything close to the house that's larger than a collie will set off an alarm. All the doors and windows have been sealed and wired. Two armed men will be inside the house at all times. Two others will be parked outside, one at curbside in front and the other alongside the garage in the rear alley. The spirit of Houdini could not breach this protective shield.

The phone rings. Aaron picks up right away. He listens, mumbles something I can't make out and hangs up. He looks at me and nods and then gets to his feet.

"Everything's set," he says, "Let's go."

I get to my feet and gather my stuff. Jill gives me a hug. Bridget holds out the baby to me and I kiss her on the forehead and then Aaron and I are out the door and on our way.

Fifteen minutes later we pull into the driveway of a small ranch home in a nicely kept residential section near Olympic and Western. Not trusting me, he gets out takng the keys, and then looks back at me.

"Don't try to run," he says.

I laugh. He laughs back and then goes inside. Ten minutes

later he emerges carrying a brown paper bag. He slides behind the wheel and dumps the bag in my lap. It's heavy. I open it up and and find a metallic blue. 45 Colt automatic.

"It's fully loaded, recently cleaned and has no parentage to get you in trouble," Aaron says. "I sure hope you know how to use it."

I smile and pull back the slide seating a bullet into the chamber. I release the clip, check it out and then slam it back into the handle In doing so I bruise my hand and let out a tiny yelp. Aaron just looks at me and shakes his head. It is said that God protects drunks and tiny babies. I'm hoping he'll expand his influence to include not-so-bright press agents.

CHAPTER NINETEEN

It's close to three o'clock when the cab pulls into my driveway. I get out gingerly. The cab driver helps me to the front door with my travel bag and the sack of groceries I picked up on the way home. I unlock the door and we go in. The cabbie drops the travel bag in the hallway and puts the groceries on my kitchen table. I pay him, including a big tip for which he thanks me effusively. I've come home by cab to give the impression of normalcy. On the very remote chance that Constable is already watching my house, I don't want to scare him off by arriving in a squad car or Aaron's unmarked Ford.

Now alone, I double check the kitchen door to the exterior, It is still bolted shut. I shrug out of my jacket and reach behind me where I have stuffed the .45 inside my belt at the small of my back. Very uncomfortable. Holsters work better. With gun in hand I make a tour of the rooms. Constable is not hiding in any of the closets and everything seems pretty much the way I left it. I raise the shades in the living room to let in the light and to give anyone outside a good look in. I know two things for sure about Byron Constable. He will not shoot me from ambush. He'll want to look me in the face when he pulls the trigger because he expects me to cringe and beg for my life. I know, too, that he has no respect for me as an adversary. Those two things give me an edge and I am going to make the most of them.

Before he let me go, Aaron asked if I had a plan other than sitting quietly like a fatted goose waiting for the hatchet. I told him I hadn't formulated anything specific. He nodded. He had suspected as much, It was then that he made an excellent suggestion. As soon as Constable is within six feet of me, I am to draw the .45 and blow a hole in him large enough to toss a football through. None of this waiting for him to draw first. That nonsense is for the likes of Hopalong Cassidy. And none of this telling him to put up his hands. I am to draw, fire and call the police. Aaron warns me that this shooting must occur within the walls of my house. This is prima facie proof of self-defense in response to a threat against my person and property. If I shoot him on the front lawn, I could get thirty years to life. It makes no sense but I tell Aaron I will remember his good counsel.

And yet.

And yet I am beginning to wonder if I have lost my mind. The firm resolve I had felt only a few hours ago is starting to melt away because in the quiet of my home where the only sound is the ticking of a clock I have no choice but to face reality. My experience with this gun I have tucked in my belt is restricted to a few hours on a practice range in the U. S. Army twelve years ago. The man who may be coming for me is a trained killer, a man who kills without compunction. Do I really have a chance against him? Has my ego or some misguided sense of duty put me in mortal danger? I am not afraid. I have chosen this plan and for better or worse I will see it through to the end but I really am questioning my sanity.

By four-thirty nothing has happened and now I wonder if I am reading Constable correctly. I'm counting on his ego to trip him up but maybe he's smarter than I think he is. No, I'm just getting impatient. I've always felt he'd strike in the dead of night. There's really no reason to think otherwise.

The phone rings. I go into the kitchen to answer it. Only Aaron knows for sure that I'm here. Maybe it's Constable checking up on me. If it is he won't say anything, he'll just hang up, but then I'll know.

I lift the receiver.

"Hello," I say.

A woman's voice.

"Mr. Bernardi, please hold for Mr. Warner."

I hold and in a minute J. L. comes on the line.

"Joe, how are you feeling? I thought I might catch you at home. Do you have help?"

Jack's an expert at asking compound questions. I'm lousy at answering them but I do my best. I'm feeling much better. The ankle's healing. No, I'm home by myself and getting along well.

"Can I expect to see you at the studio tomorrow?" he asks, having exhausted the amenities. It's not a question. It's a command.

"I can try," I say.

"Good. Your boy Dexter hasn't come up with much for the Eddie Cantor opening."

"I'll get right on it," I say.

"No need. I came up with a helluvan idea and I wanted to run it by you. There's this guy in New York name of Orlov, Orlofsky, something like that. Russian Jew. A dead ringer for Cantor. The young Cantor, not how he is now, you know what I mean? He's worked up this act, plays small time houses, charity events. We can get him for nickels and dimes."

"Why would we want to do that, Jack?" I ask.

"Because we hire him to work the street outside the theater where we open on Christmas Day. He dances, he sings, he hands out freebies for the show all first week. The papers and the television people come down to cover him. He does a little song and dance for Mom and Pop they can watch on their fucking TV sets. Maybe we have Keefe Brasselle walk by and they do a little schtick. What do you think?"

"I think it sounds good, Jack. Lots of color and it's cheap."

"That's the best part, Joe. So, will I see you tomorrow?"

"I'll be in by nine-thirty."

"See you then," Warner says and hangs up.

See you then, Jack, if I haven't died first, I think to myself.

I walk out onto my front stoop and stretch, taking in some of that cool December air. I am now wearing a very bulky, loose fitting cardigan sweater which I wear buttoned. This allows me to keep the .45 in my belt in front, undetected. The neighborhood kids are home from school now and a stickball game is underway at the other end of the block. I look around and realize that I am the only house on the block without exterior Christmas decorations. I can hear the neighbors now. Bah, humbug! The Godless One in the blue and yellow ranch. Not even a wreath on the front door. What's today? The 17th? Nine more days and I have done no shopping. None. Zero. Just the thought of all those people crowding the department stores and me on crutches is giving me the shivers. I go back inside. I must be losing my mind. I'm suddenly more nervous about Christmas shoppers than I am of Byron Constable.

Come six thirty and I heat up a can of clam chowder and toast a chicken salad sandwich. The preparation is deliberately silent. My ears are tuned for the slightest noise, anything out of the ordinary. When I go into the living room and turn on the television set I keep the volume nearly mute. I learn something interesting. There's nothing unfunnier than a television comedy show where you can't hear the jokes but everyone is dissolved in gales of laughter. I am just finishing my sandwich and downing it with V8 when I hear a familiar tinkling sound. I go to one of the living room windows and look out. The leaves in the trees are swaying to and fro and my wind chimes by the front door tell me some sort of weather is on the way.

In the kitchen I rummage around in a drawer for a couple of sturdy rubber bands, then walk out onto the front stoop and wrap the bands around the chimes rendering them silent. I look up. Dark clouds are gathering. Another storm is in the offing. I wonder if it will keep Constable away. Worse, I wonder if the noise of the wind will mask his attempt to get into the house.

I go back inside, locking the door, and resume my place on the sofa. Bing Crosby is dressed as Santa singing "White Christmas" with his family gathered around the tree. I leave the volume alone and go into the kitchen to put on a pot of coffee. No sleep tonight.

By nine o'clock I've put away three cups of coffee and sat through a muted Arthur Godfrey. The wind has picked up and the house is starting to wheeze and creak but I've heard nothing that has caused me alarm. Kraft TelevisionTheater pops onto the screen. They are presenting a truncated version of Eugene O'Neill's 'The Hairy Ape" in tribute to the playwright who died a couple of weeks ago in a hotel room in Boston. The announcer describes him as a true American treasure and a man for the ages. I couldn't agree more.

The show starts and I stare at the screen but I do not comprehend. My mind is elsewhere. I am 33, half O'Neill's age. I sum up my life. I have written one novel of which I am immensely proud. Most people who read it seemed to like it but few people actually read it. Put my book in the plus column. I served my country in war. True, I didn't carry a gun but I did what I was told and was proud and happy to do it. Another plus.

On the negative side, I have a failed marriage to answer for. I have also spent the last eight years weaving gossamer dreams out of trivialities. I have never kidded myself that what I do for a living matters very much. I know I am good at it and I'm well paid. That has been enough. But is it still enough? I think I have another book in me. Maybe several. I tell myself that I have plenty of time, that I need to mature for the words to flow effortlessly and with conviction. True? I don't know. Maybe I'm just stalling, afraid to commit, and afraid of another failure. I remember reading O'Neill's obituary a few days ago. He was 65 when he passed away but he'd quit writing ten years earlier when his Muse deserted him. Probably O'Neill thought he had a lot of time left. It must have come as a bitter shock to him to realize that all those things he had left unsaid would never be said.

I don't kid myself, I'm no Eugene O'Neill but maybe I'm a little more than a Warner Brothers flack. Maybe deep down I have something to say that might have some sort of impact on this crazy world we live in. Maybe if I put my mind to it, I could dredge up something more substantial than an Eddie Cantor lookalike singing and dancing his way outside a Broadway theater. Maybe I could do something that will force them to put something on my headstone besides "He Made Jack Warner Look Good."

Shortly past eleven I make a show of retiring for the night. I turn off the television and the living room lights and go into the bedroom. The shades are still drawn. I go to the linen closet and takes out four bath towels and bunch them up underneath the bedcovers. I'm hoping Constable falls for this ruse just long enough for me to get a shot off. I push my bedroom chair deep into a dark corner of the room, turn off the lights and raise the shades. What little light there is outside my window streams in across the bed. The trap has been baited. I sit down in the chair, the pistol in my lap and I begin to wait.

The wind continues but the rain is holding off. I hope it stays that way. To stay awake I play mind games with myself but I soon tire of it and my thoughts turn unwillingly to Bunny. In my desk drawer is Chapter One of my second book. My heroine is named Jennifer but in reality she is Bunny. The pages came hard and when I got to Chapter Two I couldn't continue. I have a feeling that deep down there is little truth in those first few pages, that I have written an idealized portrait of a woman I love and I have worked hard to hide the truth, even from myself. Jennifer is simple, Bunny is not. She is a mass of contradictions and if you asked me why I love her so deeply I would have trouble giving you a cogent answer. Maybe it isn't love at all but some sort of unreal nostalgia for the way things were, the way a perfectly happy married man of 40 will think back without good reason to a high school sweetheart and wonder what might have been.

I sit up sharply. I think I have heard a sharp noise but, no, everything is quiet. I look over at the illuminated dial of my bedroom clock. The time reads 3:21. Fear grips me. I have been asleep, an easy target. I can't let this happen. I must stay awake. I shift in my chair. Three hours to daylight and if Constable doesn't show this will all have been for nothing. For days and weeks and maybe longer Jill and Yvette will have to live in cramped circumstances with security underfoot day and night. I will be looking over my shoulder no matter where I go, praying

I'm not caught unawares by this homicidal maniac.

The minutes pass slowly. The wind has abated. Now everything is deadly quiet. Finally the first rays of morning start to steal into the bedroom. The clock reads 6:44. My elaborate charade has been for naught. Now the war begins.

I hear the phone ring in the kitchen. At this hour? Who and why? I get up and hurry out of the bedroom, .45 clutched in my hand, and make my way to the kitchen. I left the receiver.

"Yes?"

"Mr. Bernardi?"

"Yes. Who's this?"

"Willie, sir."

"Who?"

"Willie. Your paper boy. I didn't get to leave a paper this morning."

"Well, that's okay, Willie," I say.

"No, sir. I mean, I could have but I didn't because there's a man on your front stoop."

"What? What man?"

"I don't know, sir. He's just lying there. Maybe he's asleep but I don't think so. Anyway I thought you ought to know and that's why I didn't leave a paper,"

"Thanks, Willie. You did right," I say and hang up.

I walk through the living room to the front door and open it cautiously, still holding the pistol. I look down. Lying there, face buried in my welcome mat, is a dead man. I don't need to be told who it is but I kneel down anyway and turn him over. Sightless eyes stare into mine. Byron Constable's days of terrorizing his fellow man are over.

I walk back in the house and call the police. They promise that a patrol car will be on the scene shortly. Then I call Aaron

Kleinschmidt at home.

"Yeah?" he growls.

"It's me," I say.

"Are you okay?"

"Fine."

"Constable?"

"Dead."

"Good for you."

"I didn't do it."

"What?"

"I found him by my front door. Cold to the touch. He'd been dead at least two or three hours, ."

"How'd he die?"

"Shot, Aaron. Looks like a small caliber bullet to the brain. The bullet hole's at the back of hIs head, just behind his right ear."

CHAPTER TWENTY

I get to the studio by ten-thirty, thanks to a ride from Aaron. I am not quite up to driving myself. Maybe in a day or two.

Most of the morning has been chewed up with statements to the police. Pete Rodriguez was on the scene representing the Valley Division. Aaron was there for me and did his best to run interference but police procedure is fraught with delays and repetition and then more delays. By the time the meat wagon had hauled Constable off to the morgue I was hungry and testy and in no mood for chit chat. Jack Warner was expecting me at nine-thirty. I called Glenda Mae to warn Jack's secretary that I was running late but Jack Warner does not excuse tardiness by subordinates. Today has started badly. Trust me, it will only get worse.

When I talked to Aaron earlier by phone, I had asked him to check and double-check to make sure that Neville Waite actually boarded last night's plane to Heathrow. That bullet behind the ear had Waite's signature all over it. But, no, Waite is gone. Ed Lowery personally put him on the plane and BOAC confirmed that Waite passed through British Customs over an hour ago.

When I walk into the office, Glenda Mae claims to be glad to see me but she doesn't like the looks of my taped ankle or my crutches. Good thing she can't see through my shirt to the bandage on my arm or the tape wrapped tightly around my rib cage. I'd be on the wrong end of an interminable lecture and I have yet to devise a way to shut her up when she gets on one of her rants. She has already gone through my mail over the past several days, deemed most of it unworthy of my attention and personally responded to anything that looked reasonably important. Since she can sign my name more legibly than I can, I feel I am safely covered. There is only one thing of importance outstanding and that's a phone call from Lou Cioffi at the Times. He said it was important and I'm told his tone of voice reeked of acute indigestion.

"What the hell are you trying to pull, Bernardi?" he seethes when he comes on the line and I'm pretty sure if I looked, I'd see smoke billowing out of the earpiece.

"Don't know what you mean, Lou," I say.

"The hell you don't," Lou says. "Where's this front page story you were so hot to tell me about?"

"I'm still lost," I say helplessly.

"The London Daily Mail. The byline story by this guy named Finch? Hey, old pal, there is no story. Not on Monday and not on Tuesday. Nothing."

"That can't be," I say.

"That do be," he says sarcastically. "Did you sucker me, Joe? Is that it?"

"No, Lou. Swear to God. I'll have to get back to you."

"Yeah, sure," he says, believing me like he believes in fairy dust.

But then I hesitate, thinking I may be the one who got suckered. I say, "Lou, you got a pencil?"

"I'm a reporter," he says. "I always got a pencil."

"Write this down. Movie producer Byron Constable was found shot to death on the front steps of Warner Brothers executive Joseph Bernardi's home early this morning. No motive for the shooting has been established. Detective Sergeant Pedro Rodriguez of the Van Nuys Division is heading up the investigation with the help of homicide Detective Sergeant Aaron Kleinschmidt. Among the eyewitnesses to the police activity was Bernardi's next door neighbor Charles Bledsoe."

There is a long silence and then Lou says, "Are you kidding me?"

"You've got enough to start. Go write it and if my two favorite cops try to stonewall you, Chuck Bledsoe knows most of it."

"Forget what I said, Joe," Lou says sheepishly.

"And you forget you ever talked to me," I say.

"You're forgotten already," Lou says gleefully and hangs up.

"Glenda Mae!" I shout through my open doorway.

In a moment she appears with a disapproving look on her face.

"My, aren't we in a mood," she says.

"I was expecting some faxes sent from London by a woman named Sheila Noone. Have you got them?"

"No."

"Would you check the mail room and see if they came in," I say.

She waits.

"Please," I add.

"Certainly, my lord and master. And next time, please use the intercom. That's the tone of voice I use to call my cat."

I smile shamefacedly.

"Sorry."

She disappears. In two minutes she's back.

"No faxes," she says.

"Are they sure?"

"Positive," she replies. "About this girl Noone. There's another way to pronounce n-o-o-n-e. Try no one."

I look at her and it dawns on me.

"Son of a bitch," I mutter.

"I'll be at my desk," she says and leaves the doorway. I am about to scream her name again but catch myself in time. I buzz her on the intercom.

"I need the number for the London Daily Mail," I say softly.

"I have it right here," she replies. "I called it just the other day."

"No, get me the REAL number and find out what the editor's name is. And Glenda Mae, darling, chop chop." That means I needed it an hour ago and in our little private world of code words, this is Priority One. No joke. No stalling. Get on it NOW.

Twenty minutes later I am talking to Andrew Humphreys, managing editor of the London Daily Mail. Lou was right. There was no story of any kind about the murder of Ivor Willoughby. And, as I suspected, Humphreys has never heard of Alexander Finch. As soon as I hang up I ask Glenda Mae to get me the desk clerk at the Shamrock Motel on Ventura Boulevard in Studio City. The clerk is an eager to please young man who tells me that Finch checked out shortly before ten o'clock to catch a flight back to London. He believes the plane is scheduled to take off around one p. m. and Finch left early to return his rental car.

I hang up and call Vic Perini direct. Vic is the transportation captain on the picture and when I tell him I need a ride to the airport immediately, he doesn't argue with me. Carting around studio executives on their personal business does not fall within the parameters of the Teamsters contract but Vic's a common sense guy and he knows me well enough to know I wouldn't ask if it weren't important. He may also know I am a walking invalid.

As I head out the door, informing Glenda Mae where I'll be, she asks what she should do if Warner calls. "Tell him we'll have to do it later this afternoon."

"He won't like it," she says.

I borrow a line from Gable.

"Frankly, my dear, I don't give a damn."

And then I'm out the door and down the hallway.

I reach the bottom of the outside staircase one slow step at a time just as Vic pulls up in a new Lincoln Continental. I open the front passenger door, and toss the crutches in the back seat and slide in next to Vic.

"Nice wheels," I say.

"Mr. Milland's. He's away for a few days."

Ray Milland's on the lot shooting "Dial M for Murder" for Hitchcock. Part of his deal is he gets taken to and from the studio by a studio driver in a studio car. Today his car is mine. Vic's a good natured chatty guy and I ask him how it's going on the set. Good, he says, and that's high praise coming from a Teamster. The drivers always know what's going on and they can tell instinctively if the film they're working on is a winner or a washout. Vic says this one's going to be a moneymaker, no question about it. Jack Warner will be glad to hear it.

I check my watch as we turn onto Century Boulevard. 11:45. The International terminal is down near the end. We're cutting it close. I don't know how early BOAC starts to board but it's got to be at least thirty minutes before takeoff. Vic skids to a halt in front of the terminal. I get out and grab my crutches. I tell Vic to go back to the studio. I'll catch a cab when I'm done here. He nods and drives off and I start to hobble toward the main entrance.

It takes fifteen minutes to get to the BOAC first class lounge and another five minutes to b. s. my way past the receptionist who is severely distraught that I am not a ticketed passenger, . However, once again my Warner Brothers credentials batter down the barricade and as soon as I enter the spacious and airy waiting area, I find Alexander Finch on a sofa off in a corner, an open attache case on his lap, going over some papers. He doesn't notice me until I am hovering over him.

"Not a single word of goodbye. I'm hurt," I say.

He looks up and there's no question, he's startled to see me. Startled and none too pleased if I read him correctly.

"Mr. Bernardi, how nice to see you," he says, trying to cover his annoyance, even as he skillfully slips his paperwork into the case and closes the lid.

"Well, I couldn't very well let you fly off without a word of thanks for all you've done for me."

A dismissive shrug.

"It was nothing."

"Oh, no," I say sitting down in the chair opposite him. "All those details, that background material on Smythe-James, the lowdown on Neville Waite. Honestly, Mr. Finch, you were invaluable."

"As I said, nothing really. We journalists have to stick together. Maybe someday you can return the favor."

"Say the word, Mr. Finch. Whatever you need. An interview with the great Jack Warner, luncheon with Alfred Hitchcock, the sex secrets of Laurel and Hardy, a dead body dropped on your front porch early some morning."

I watch for a reaction and I get it. For one fleeting instant I see it in his eyes and then he lowers the curtain.

"Stan and Ollie sound interesting. Maybe you could fax me some details. Pictures if you have them."

"Be happy to. I'll shoot them over to Sheila Noone while your plane's in the air. They'll be on her desk before you touch down at Heathrow. Do you have a fax number for her or should I just send everything to MI6 to her attention?"

Finch leans back, lacing his hands behind his neck as he regards me with a curious smile.

"Have I underestimated you, Mr. Bernardi? I think perhaps I have."

"Maybe so. By the way, you clean up very well. Freshly washed hair, a tailored suit, no more jagged stained teeth and whatever happened to that ludicrous working class accent you were fabricating?"

He shakes his head sadly.

"I always have trouble with it. Not quite Cockney, not quite Lambeth, I should really chuck it, don't you think?:"

"Up to you. Anyway, thanks for neutralizing Constable for me. I can breathe easier now. So can Jillian."

"It was a privilege," Finch says.

"Just out of curiosity, may I ask the how and the why?"

A female voice comes over the lounge's sound system.

"All passengers for Flight 34 departing at 1:10 for Heathrow, this your first call. First call for Flight 34 departing at 1:10 from Gate 11."

Finch checks his watch and then looks up at me.

"As to the why, Waite had already left London when my superiors got around to reviewing the Willoughby file. Two things struck them. One was Waite's overt animosity toward Willoughby for disappearing back in '48. Waite holds grudges and it clouds his judgement. Second was all that business with Smythe-James, the Canadian traitor. We knew Willoughby was obsessed with bringing him to justice and there was a chance, a slim one, that maybe he had stumbled onto something. Also, by this time, we had a new head of the service who had been a pilot during the war and spent eleven months as a prisoner. If there was a chance that we could run Smythe-James to ground, he was for it so a day after Waite flew to Los Angeles, I followed him."

"And Alexander Finch, ace reporter for the Daily Mail?"

He shrugs.

"I prefer to come into a situation sideways. I find that strutting about and announcing oneself as an operative for MI6 is not always the most productive way to get results."

"You have no use for Nevlle Waite."

"Never have. Never will," Finch says. "I tolerate him because I must."

"And all that hyperbole about Waite's background and tactics?"

"Mostly true. He would have fit in nicely in Queen Victoria's court but in my opinion he is woefully out of place in post-war Britain. We are no longer rulers of the sea. The empire has shrunk and the dominions like Canada and Australia do pretty much what they please without the blessing of parliament or the Queen. We are a war ravaged little island in danger of becoming irrelevant in the world picture and still Waite deludes himself that a return to the days of glory is but a year or two away. Still, he was one of the first to be recruited and no one has the heart to sack him so we cover for him."

I nod. Tradition. Loyalty. Appearances. All these are part of the British psyche. I don't doubt Finch for a moment.

"And the how?" I ask.

"I'd heard about the angry threats Constable had made against you at the police lineup and when I learned he'd made bail. I knew right away you were in danger. Then when I heard that you had moved back into your house alone, crippled, I thought you'd lost your mind. As soon as it was dark I hung around your place, watching you, and I realized immediately that you were baiting a trap, especially when I got a look at that. 45 you had stuck in your belt. Did you really think you could take on a man like Constable, mano a mano?"

"Absolutely."

"Well, I admire your courage if not your intelligence. That's when I decided to stick around all night. Against Constable, I had a far better chance than you did. When he finally showed up around three in the morning, It was a simple matter of quietly leaving my hiding place, putting the barrel of my. 32 caliber revolver behind his ear and pulling the trigger."

"I am grateful, Mr. Finch," I say, "but you do understand that in the eyes of my government you are guilty of murder."

He nods.

"Yes, I'm sure," he says. "A month ago my beautiful garden was being destroyed by a pesky rabbit with a big appetite so I laid in wait and when he appeared, I murdered him to save my garden from further ruination. The only difference between that rabbit and Constable is, I didn't eat Mr. Constable for dinner.

The feminine voice comes back on the loudspeaker system and announces the final call for Flight 34 for London. Finch stands and extends his hand to me. I take it and we shake.

"It's been a pleasure, Mr. Bernardi. If ever you get to London, please look me up. I'm not in the book for obvious reasons but if you ring up MI6, they can get a message to me. Oh, and don't ask for Alexander Finch. They'll deny knowing me. Ask for

Meriwether Mallory."

"I'll remember it," I say. "Is that your real name?"

He shakes his head.

"Oh, I see," I say. "Then Alexander Finch is actually—"

He shakes his head again.

"Goodbye, Mr. Bernardi. Goodbye and good luck."

And he walks off toward the exit.

I watch him go and I remember something Waite had said to me, that he and a few other clandestine agents had permission from the government to kill enemies of the Crown without the inconvenience of a trial. I find it hard to believe even though the proof was lying on my front stoop at daybreak. A license to kill. It sounds like something out of a bad spy novel.

CHAPTER TWENTY ONE

The cab drops me off at the bottom of the staircase. Since leaving the airport I've done a lot of thinking and I conclude that I am a very lucky man. Whoever Alexander Finch may be, he has saved my life. More importantly, he's eliminated the threat to Jill and Yvette. This will truly be a Christmas season worth celebrating. I overtip the driver shamelessly even as I vow to shop later today for a tree and Christmas lights. The spirit is with me and I smile all the way to my office.

"Mr. Warner is on the warpath," Glenda Mae says to me grimly as I hobble into the office. So much for goodwill toward men.

"I'd better get this over with," I say, starting to turn around.

She reaches for the phone.

"Shall I check to see if he's available?"

I shake my head.

"If he's not I'll just wait."

"Might be quite a while."

"I can handle it."

"I see. Self-flaggelation. Can I get you something to take along? Hair shirt, perhaps. Crown of thorns?"

"Don't need them," I say. "I'm going to prostrate myself on

his carpet and hope for the best."

"Good luck," she smiles.

Actually, Jack sees me right away and he's more concerned than angry. By now he has heard about the demise of Byron Constable on my front stoop and he wants to make sure I'm okay.

"A helluva thing," Warner says, shaking his head. "He was there planning to kill you, did I hear that right?" He's smoking one of those expensive but noxious cigars he's so fond of and his office is redolent with barnyard odors.

I told him that he had heard correctly and I gave him the short version of Constable's real identity and the fact that he had tortured and murdered the man we had known as Wiley Wyckham.

More head shaking.

"Well, the important thing is that you're okay, Joe. How soon before you can ditch those walking sticks?" he asks pointing to my crutches.

"Maybe a week," I say.

He nods.

"Look, I hate to do this to you after all you've been through, but I'm going to need you in New York."

"For how long?"

"At least ten days. I want this Eddie Cantor thing handled right and I can't trust anyone else."

"Ten days will put me away from home for Christmas."

"I know. Can't be helped. Sombody's got to deal with at least a dozen newspapers, five or six TV stations, all those radio outlets. I can't trust this to your boy Dexter, not yet."

"I disagree, Jack. He's come a long way."

"But he's not there yet, Joe. No, this is your baby. I'm counting on you."

"How about if we retain one of those high powered New York publicity firms to fill in? I hear good things about PR Newswire. I know they've got the contacts—'

"You're not hearing me, Joe. I want you on this. No one else."

I hesitate.

"All right. I'll fly out tomorrow with Dexter. Get everything set up. Contracts, permits, everything in place and then fly back on the 24th. Dexter can handle the rest."

Jack's eyes narrow. He doesn't like pushback and that's what he's getting. He jabs at me with what's left of his cigar.

"The picture opens Christmas Day. I want you there."

I pause carefully. I'm at the edge of the precipice, staring down into the chasm. I need time to make a rational decision but time's the one thing I haven't got.

"Sorry, J. L. I can't do it," I finally hear myself say.

He glares at me.

"Can't do it? What are you talking about?"

"I have plans for Christmas Day," I tell him.

"Change them."

"Can't do it."

"Don't you mean, won't do it?"

"Either way," I say.

He glowers at me, then realizes that his cigar has gone dead. Annoyed he relights it and blows a huge cloud of smoke into the air.

"We've had this discussion before."

"Yes, we have," I say.

"The studio comes first."

"Not any more. I'm actually trying to have a life."

"Do you want me to fire you, is that it?" Warner asks.

"Look, Jack," I say, "you've been good to me for almost seven years. You've treated me with respect and always been square with me, even when we disagreed. I accepted your bellowing because I knew that deep down, what mattered most to you was the welfare of this studio and the cursing wasn't personal. But I've reached the point in my life where other things are claiming my attention and they can't be ignored. I know who you are, Jack. I know what makes you tick and it's not enough that I work for you diligently and loyally, you must also own me and I can no longer let you do that."

I stand up and stare down at him.

"You'll have my resignation by the end of the day."

He stares back at me and then he waves his cigar toward my chair.

"Oh, sit down, Joe. You want to be back for Christmas, fine. Come back for Christmas."

"No," I say."It's too late for that. We'd be having this conversation next month and the month after that. Let's make the break now, Jack, and part on good terms."

"You've got a contract," he says icily.

"No, I don't. You always refused to give me one."

That stops him cold but just for a moment.

"I can have you blackballed by every studio in town," he says.

"No, you can't. I can think of three studio heads who would hire me this afternoon just to spite you." I lean across the desk. "Come on, Jack, we've been through too much to end up spitting at each other. I'm going to be around a long time and so are you. If ever you need something from me, just pick up the phone and no matter what else I'm doing, I'll be there for you. My word on it."

I put out my hand. He looks at it as if it were leperous. Finally he gets up from his chair, grabs my hand and gives it a firm shake.

"No severance pay," he growls.

"I didn't expect any," I say.

"All right, six weeks, but you drive a hard bargain. Now get out of here."

I give him a smile and hobble out.

Jack L. Warner, well known scrooge and studio tough guy. If his naysayers only knew.

I'm back to my office and as I clump my way past Glenda Mae I ask her to get me Bertha Bowles. This seems like an ideal time to find out if the lady is a player or mostly hot air. As I sit behind my desk, I revise my estimate of the people who would hire me just to rub Jack's nose in it. I can count to one but I'm unenthused. Truth be told, I wouldn't go to work for Harry Cohn if I were reduced to eating kibble and Alpo. Harry's the kind of studio boss that gives tyrants like Vlad the Impaler a bad name.

Glenda Mae buzzes me. I pick up.

"Bertha," I say.

"Good. You're alive," she says. "You hear so many rumors you never know. How are you feeling?"

"Feisty," I say.

"Feisty as in rebellious?" she asks.

"You could say that. Our chat from the other day, is that proposal still on the table?"

"Are we talking here about Bernardi & Bowles?"

"I prefer it the other way around," I say. "Ladies first."

"I can live with that. What's Jack have to say for himself?"

"Not much. He gets my resignation this afternoon. I'm outta here, effective immediately."

"He can't be happy."

"He's not but he's resigned and we're parting on good terms."

"There's a first. Jack doesn't usually let the talent push him around. Just ask Bette Davis."

"Nevertheless, that's the way it is."

"Well, I couldn't be more delighted. What are you doing for dinner?" Bertha asks.

"What did you have in mind?"

"A celebration at the Polo Lounge. Lobsters and caviar, gallons of champagne, all topped off with a hundred year old brandy."

"I could do that," I say. "My tab," I add.

I look up as Dexter bursts into the room, a grin on his face that would make Joe E. Brown look tight-lipped. I hold up my hand and he freezes in place.

"No, it's on me," she says.

"My tab or I don't show up," I say resolutely.

"In that case," Bertha says. "Eight o'clock sharp."

"I'll be there, partner," I say and hang up. I look up at Dexter who, while motionless, is still grinning.

"I got Eddie Cantor," he says bubbling over with excitement. . "Mr. Warner gave me Eddie Cantor."

"Wow!" I say.

"I leave for New York tomorrow. I'm going to be there over the holidays."

"Wow again," I say.

"I know you did this for me, Joe, and I want you to know I am really grateful."

"No, it was all Mr. Warner's idea. I told him you would bust your butt for him and he believed me."

"Oh, I will, Joe. Absolutely."

"Good man. Now go home and pack, Dexter. New York may

be a fairyland at Christmastime but it's also colder than a penguin's balls so dress warm."

"Gotcha."

"Do you need a couple of phone numbers? A young good looking single guy like you shouldn't spend the holidays alone in a big city."

He shakes his head.

"I'll be fine."

"You sure?"

"Sure. And thanks again, Joe."

He turns and hurries from the room. Just as I once worried that I might turn out to be another Charlie Berger, now I worry that this eager young kid may turn out to be me. Well, I think, on balance, he could do worse.

I reach over to the phone and buzz the intercom, then look up. She's already standing in the doorway.

"You rang?" Glenda Mae says.

"Yes, I need you to—"

I might just as well have saved my breath. She strides to the desk and lays down a single sheet of paper for my signature. It's my resignation.

I frown at her.

"You were listening on the phone."

She shakes her head, .

"You were talking loudly,"

"Not that loudly, Sit down. We need to talk."

She sits.

"When do we start?" she asks.

"What?"

"Bowles & Bernardi. When do we start?"

"Oh, no," I say firmly.

"Oh, yes," she replies just as firmly. "You're going to need a secretary. I'm available."

"No, no. You have a secure future here, Glenda Mae, not to mention your pension."

"My pension is with the union, not Warner Brothers, and I, too, have no contract. What's more if things don't work out, with my skills, I can get a job anywhere in town in the blink of an eyelash and incidentally, I've discovered that the blinking of an eyelash is a big help."

I stare at her. She stares back.

Finally I say, "I know that your husband Beau will eat anything that doesn't bite back but how does he feel about really fine gourmet food?"

She shrugs.

"I don't know," she says. "I don't believe he's ever had any."

I nod.

"Okay. Tonight. You and Beau. The Polo Lounge. Eight o'clock. And tell Beau to wear a tie."

THE END

AUTHOR'S NOTE

"Has Anybody Here Seen Wyckham" is (obviously) a work of fiction and while the members of the cast and crew of "The High and the Mighty" were real, all other characters are the creation of the author. Scenes that include dialogue with John Wayne and other cast members as well as studio head Jack Warner are total fiction. During the 1970s, a series of "Airport" pictures was produced, starting with the original based on a novel by Arthur Hailey. All of these pictures basically followed the template pioneered by "The High and the Mighty" which was a huge financial success as well as garnering rave reviews from a majority of the country's most influential critics. Released in July of 1954. It was nominated for six Academy Awards (including Best Supporting Actress nods for both Claire Trevor and Jan Sterling) but won only for Best Original Music Score by Dimitri Tiomkin. In accepting his Oscar Tiomkin took pains to thank all those who had helped him win including Bach, Beethoven and Tchaikowsky. A television staple well into the 1980's, the film disappeared for nearly twenty years before being restored to its original grandeur by the Wayne estate and is currently available on DVD along with its predecessor and "companion" movie, "Island In The Sky", an airplane movie also starring John Wayne, directed by William Wellman and based on a novel by Ernest Gann.

MISSING SOMETHING?

The first eight books in the Hollywood Murder Mystery series are now available from Grove Point Press. All copies will be personally signed and dated by the author. If you purchase ANY THREE for $29.85, you automatically become a member of "the club". This means that you will be able to buy any and all volumes in any quantity at the $9.95 price, a savings of $3.00 over the regular cover price of $12.95. This offer is confined to direct purchases from The Grove Point Press and does not apply to other on-line sites which may carry the series.

Book One—1947

JEZEBEL IN BLUE SATIN

WWII is over and Joe Bernardi has just returned home after three years as a war correspondent in Europe. Married in the heat of passion three weeks before he shipped out, he has come home to find his wife Lydia a complete stranger. It's not long before Lydia is off to Reno for a quickie divorce which Joe won't accept. Meanwhile he's been hired as a publicist by third rate movie studio, Continental Pictures. One night he enters a darkened sound stage only to discover the dead body of ambitious, would-be actress Maggie Baumann. When the police investigate, they immediately zero in on Joe as the perp. Short on evidence they attempt to frame him and almost succeed. Who really killed Maggie? Was it the over-the-hill actress trying for a comeback? Or the talentless director with delusions of grandeur? Or maybe it was the hapless leading man whose career is headed nowhere now that the "real stars" are coming back from the war. There is no shortage of suspects as the story speeds along to its exciting and unexpected conclusion.

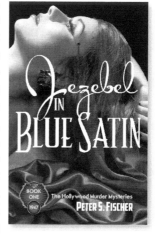

$12.95 (9.95 to Club Members)

Book Two—1948
WE DON'T NEED NO STINKING BADGES

Joe Bernardi is the new guy in Warner Brothers' Press Department so it's no surprise when Joe is given the unenviable task of flying to Tampico, Mexico, to bail Humphrey Bogart out of jail without the world learning about it. When he 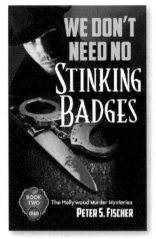 arrives he discovers that Bogie isn't the problem. So-called accidents are occurring daily on the set, slowing down the filming of "The Treasure of the Sierra Madre" and putting tempers on edge. Everyone knows who's behind the sabotage. It's the local Jefe who has a finger in every illegal pie. But suddenly the intrigue widens and the murder of one of the actors throws the company into turmoil. Day by day, Joe finds himself drawn into a dangerous web of deceit, dupliciity and blackmail that nearly costs him his life.

$12.95 (9.95 to Club Members)

Book Three—1949
LOVE HAS NOTHING TO DO WITH IT

Joe Bernardi's ex-wife Lydia is in big, big trouble. On a Sunday evening around midnight she is seen running from the plush offices of her one- time lover, Tyler Banks. She disappears into the night leaving Banks behind, dead on the carpet with a bullet in his head. Convinced that she is innocent, Joe enlists the help of his pal, lawyer Ray Giordano, and bail bondsman Mick Clausen, to prove Lydia's innocence, even as his assignment to publicize Jimmy Cagney's comeback movie for Warner's threatens to take up all of his time. Who really pulled the trigger that night? Was it the millionaire whose influence reached into City Hall? Or the not so grieving widow finally freed from a loveless marriage. Maybe it was the partner who wanted

the business all to himself as well as the new widow. And what about the mysterious envelope, the one that disappeared and everyone claims never existed? Is it the key to the killer's identity and what is the secret that has been kept hidden for the past forty years? *$12.95 (9.95 to Club Members)*

Book Four—1950
EVERYBODY WANTS AN OSCAR

After six long years Joe Bernardi's novel is at last finished and has been shipped to a publisher. But even as he awaits news, fingers crossed for luck, things are heating up at the studio. Soon production will begin on Tennessee Williams' "The Glass Menagerie" and Jane Wyman has her sights set on a second consecutive Academy Award. Jack Warner has just signed Gertrude Lawrence for the pivotal role of Amanda and is positive that the Oscar will go to Gertie. And meanwhile Eleanor Parker, who has gotten rave reviews for a prison picture called "Caged" is sure that 1950 is her year to take home the trophy. Faced with three very talented ladies all vying for his best efforts, Joe is resigned to performing a monumental juggling act. Thank God 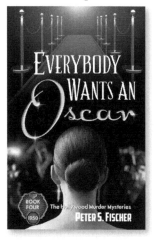 he has nothing else to worry about or at least that was the case until his agent informed him that a screenplay is floating around Hollywood that is a dead ringer for his newly completed novel. Will the ladies be forced to take a back seat as Joe goes after the thief that has stolen his work, his good name and six years of his life? *$12.95 (9.95 to Club Members)*

Book Five—1951
THE UNKINDNESS OF STRANGERS

Warner Brothers is getting it from all sides and Joe Bernardi seems to be everybody's favorite target. "A Streetcar Named Desire" is unproducible, they say. Too violent, too seedy, too sexy, too controversial and what's worse, it's being directed by that well-known pinko, Elia Kazan. To make matters worse, the country's number one hate monger, newspaper columnist Bryce Tremayne, is coming after Kazan with a vengeance and nothing Joe can do or say will stop him. A vicious expose column is set to run in every Hearst paper in the nation on the upcoming Sunday but a funny thing happens Friday night. Tremayne is found in a compromising condition behind the wheel of his car, a bullet hole between his eyes. Come Sunday and the scurrilous attack on Kazan does not appear. Rumors fly. Kazan is suspected but he's not the only one with a motive. Consider:

Elvira Tremayne, the unloved widow. Did Tremayne slug her one time too many?

Hubbell Cox, the flunky whose homosexuality made him a target of derision.

Willie Babbitt, the muscle. He does what he's told and what he's told to do is often unpleasant.

Jenny Coughlin, Tremayne's private secretary. But how private and what was her secret agenda?

Jed Tompkins, Elvira's father, a rich Texas cattle baron who had only contempt for his son-in-law.

Boyd Larabee, the bookkeeper, hired by Tompkins to win Cox's confidence and report back anything he's learned.

Annie Petrakis, studio makeup artist. Tremayne destroyed her lover. Has she returned the favor?

$12.95 (9.95 to Club Members)

Book Six—1952
NICE GUYS FINISH DEAD

Ned Sharkey is a fugitive from mob revenge. For six years he's been successfully hiding out in the Los Angeles area while a $100, 000 contract for his demise hangs over his head. But when Warner Brothers begins filming "The Winning Team", the story of Grover Cleveland Alexander, Ned can't resist showing up at the ballpark to reunite with his old pals from the Chicago Cubs of the early 40's who have cameo roles in the film. Big mistake. When Joe Bernardi, Warner Brothers publicity guy, inadvertently sends a press release and a photo of Ned to the Chicago papers, mysterious people from the Windy City suddenly appear and a day later at break of dawn, Ned's body is found sprawled atop the pitcher's mound. It appears that 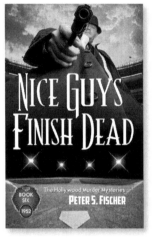 someone is a hundred thousand dollars richer. Or maybe not. Who is the 22 year old kid posing as a 50 year old former hockey star? And what about Gordo Gagliano, a mountain of a man, who is out to find Ned no matter who he has to hurt to succeed? And why did baggy pants comic Fats McCoy jump Ned and try to kill him in the pool parlor? It sure wasn't about money. Joe , riddled with guilt because the photo he sent to the newspapers may have led to Ned's death, finds himself embroiled in a dangerous game of who-dun-it that leads from L. A. 's Wrigley Field to an upscale sports bar in Altadena to the posh mansions of Pasadena and finally to the swank clubhouse of Santa Anita racetrack.
$12.95 (9.95 to Club Members)

Book Seven—1953
PRAY FOR US SINNERS

Joe finds himself in Quebec but it's no vacation. Alfred Hitchcock is shooting a suspenseful thriller called "I Confess" and Montgomery Clift is playing a priest accused of murder. A marriage made in heaven? Hardly. They have been at log- 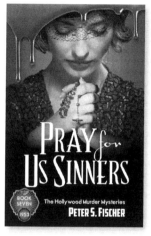 gerheads since Day One and to make matters worse their feud is spilling out into the newspapers. When viva- cious Jeanne d'Arcy, the director of the Quebec Film Commisssion volunteers to help calm the troubled waters, Joe thinks his troubles are over but that was before Jeanne got into a violent spat with a for- mer lover and suddenly found herself under arrest on a charge of first degree murder. Guilty or not guilty? Half the clues say she did it, the other half say she is being brilliantly framed. But by who? Fingers point to the crooked Gonsalvo brothers who have ties to the Buffalo mafia family and when Joe gets too close to the truth, someone tries to shut him up. . . permanently. With the Archbishop threatening to shut down the production in the wake of the scandal, Joe finds himself torn between two loyalties.

$12.95 (9.95 to Club Members)

Everything was going smoothly on the set of "The High and the Mighty" until the cast and crew returned from lunch. With one exception. Wiley Wyckham, the bit player sitting in seat 24A on the airliner mockup, is among the missing, and without Wyckham sitting in place, director William Wellman cannot continue filming, A studio wide search is instituted. No Wyckham. A lookalike is hired that night, filming resumes the next day and still no Wyckham. Except that by this time, it's been discovered that Wyckham, a British actor, isn't really Wyckham at all but an imposter who may very well be an agent for the Russian government, The local police call in the FBI. The FBI calls in British counterintel-ligence. A manhunt for the missing actor

ensues and Joe Bernardi, the picture's publicist, is right in the middle of the intrigue. Everyone's upset, especially John Wayne who is furious to learn that a possible Commie spy has been working in a picture he's producing and starring in. And then they find him . It's the dead of night on the Warner Brothers backlot and Wyckham is discovered hanging by his feet from a streetlamp, his body blood-ied and tortured and very much dead. and pinned to his shirt is a piece of paper with the inscription "Sic Semper Proditor". (Thus to all traitors). Who was this man who had been posing as an obscure British actor? How did he smuggle himself into the country and what has he been up to? Has he been blackmailing an important higher-up in the film business and did the victim suddenly turn on him? Is the MI6 agent from London really who he says he is and what about the reporter from the London Daily Mail who seems to know all the right questions to ask as well all the right answers. *$12.95 (9.95 to Club Members)*

ABOUT THE AUTHOR

Peter S. Fischer is a former television writer-producer who currently lives with his wife Lucille in the Monterey Bay area of Central California. He is a co-creator of "Murder, She Wrote" for which he wrote over 40 scripts. Among his other credits are a dozen "Columbo" episodes and a season helming "Ellery Queen". He has also written and produced several TV mini-series and Movies of the Week. In 1985 he was awarded an Edgar by the Mystery Writers of America. "Has Anybody Here Seen Wyckham?" is the eighth in a series of murder mysteries set in post WWII Hollywood and featuring publicist and would-be novelist, Joe Bernardi.

TO PURCHASE COPIES OF THE HOLLYWOOD MURDER MYSTERIES. . .

Check first with your local book seller. If he is out of stock or is unable to order copies for you, go online to Amazon Books where every volume in the series is available either as a paperback or in the Kindle format.

Alternatively, you may wish to order paperback editions direct from the publisher, The Grove Point Press, P. O. Box 873, Pacific Grove, CA 93950. Each copy purchased directly will be signed by the author and personalized, if desired. If your initial order is for three or more different titles, your price per copy drops to $9.95 and you automatically become a member of the "club." Club members may purchase any or all titles in any quantity, all for the same low price of $9.95 each. In addition, all those ordering direct from the publisher will receive a FREE "Murder, She Wrote" bookmark personally autographed by the author.

TURN TO THE NEXT PAGE

for the easy-to-use order form.

Want to know more about
THE HOLLYWOOD MURDER MYSTERIES?
click on
THEGROVEPOINTPRESS.COM

ORDER FORM

To
THE GROVE POINT PRESS
P. O. Box 873
Pacific Grove, CA 93950

☐ Please send the volume(s), either one or two, checked below at $12.95 each. I understand each copy will be signed personally by the author. Also include my FREE "Murder, She Wrote" keepsake bookmark, also autographed by the author.

☐ Please send the volumes checked below (three or more) at the low price of $9.95 each. I understand this entitles me to any and all future purchases at this same low price. I also understand that each volume will be personally signed by the author. Also include my FREE "Murder, She Wrote" keepsake bookmark, also autographed by the author.

QTY

_____ *Book One—1947* **Jezebel in Blue Satin**

_____ *Book Two—1948* **We Don't Need No Stinking Badges**

_____ *Book Three—1949* **Love Has Nothing to Do With It**

_____ *Book Four—1950* **Everybody Wants An Oscar**

_____ *Book Five—1951* **The Unkindess of Strangers**

_____ *Book Six—1952* **Nice Guys Finish Dead**

_____ *Book Seven—1953* **Pray For Us Sinners**

_____ *Book Eight—1954* **Has Anybody Here Seen Wyckham?**

NAME _____

STREET ADDRESS _____

CITY _____

STATE _____ ZIP _____

Enclosed find in the amount of _____ for a total of _____ volumes. I understand there are no shipping and handling charges and that any taxes will be paid by the publisher.

✂

ORDER FORM

To
THE GROVE POINT PRESS
P. O. Box 873
Pacific Grove, CA 93950

☐ Please send the volume(s), either one or two, checked below at $12.95 each. I understand each copy will be signed personally by the author. Also include my FREE "Murder, She Wrote" keepsake bookmark, also autographed by the author.

☐ Please send the volumes checked below (three or more) at the low price of $9.95 each. I understand this entitles me to any and all future purchases at this same low price. I also understand that each volume will be personally signed by the author. Also include my FREE "Murder, She Wrote" keepsake bookmark, also autographed by the author.

QTY

_____ *Book One—1947* **Jezebel in Blue Satin**

_____ *Book Two—1948* **We Don't Need No Stinking Badges**

_____ *Book Three—1949* **Love Has Nothing to Do With It**

_____ *Book Four—1950* **Everybody Wants An Oscar**

_____ *Book Five—1951* **The Unkindess of Strangers**

_____ *Book Six—1952* **Nice Guys Finish Dead**

_____ *Book Seven—1953* **Pray For Us Sinners**

_____ *Book Eight—1954* **Has Anybody Here Seen Wyckham?**

NAME _____

STREET ADDRESS _____

CITY _____

STATE _____ **ZIP** _____

Enclosed find in the amount of _____ for a total of _____ volumes. I understand there are no shipping and handling charges and that any taxes will be paid by the publisher.